SECOND CHANCES IN WILLOW HEIGHTS

WILLOW HEIGHTS SERIES BOOK NINE

ABIGAIL BECK

CHAPTER 1

*L*orraine stood in the middle of her empty home, her eyes sparkling with pride and joy. She looked around at the freshly painted walls, the brand-new stainless-steel appliances, and the hardwood floors. She couldn't believe this place was finally hers and that she could provide it for herself and Wyatt. Lorraine took a deep breath and looked at the small stack of boxes holding her belongings in the room's corner. This home might be small compared to other homes, but this was the largest home she'd ever lived in.

The home had two bedrooms and two bathrooms. She had been saving up for some time and was happy to see things coming together. Thomas and Mary Elle helped her come up with a small down payment for the home. Mrs. Klein, her realtor, helped her find programs that helped low-income homebuyers. Lorraine was still in disbelief that she had people in her life who believed in her and wanted to see her succeed. After many years of living in uncertainty, never knowing how she would get by, she finally felt like she was in a good place in her life.

Later today, a delivery would arrive with a bed, a dresser, and a desk for Wyatt's room. Even though he would go to college soon, she wanted him to know he had a place to stay with her. Lorraine wished more than anything that she could've provided more for Wyatt growing up. She wished she could've been a better example to him, but there was no going back now; all she could focus on was their future.

Unable to stay still, Lorraine cleaned the already clean house. As she walked from room to room, she envisioned her life here. Lorraine thought of all the beautiful memories she would create here with Wyatt. She wondered where they could put the Christmas tree in the living room. She imagined baking with him in the kitchen like they had when he was younger.

Lorraine stepped out onto her front porch and looked out into the street. Tall trees lined the street, and the air was crisp and cool. The scent of pine trees and wildflowers filled the air. In the distance, she could hear the creek rushing over the rocks and the birds chirping away. A sense of peace rushed over as she took it all in. She still couldn't believe that she had really done it. She wasn't dreaming. This was real life. When she set out to buy a house, it felt like such an unattainable task, but her wish had come true, and she knew now that she could accomplish anything she set her mind to.

Just then, a moving truck pulled into her driveway. She didn't think the delivery would be until later in the afternoon. She wasn't expecting anyone right now. Lorraine walked over to the truck and smiled when she saw Mary Elle and Thomas jumping out of the truck.

"Welcome to my humble adobe!" she said.

"I hope we're not interrupting you. I tried to tell Mary Elle that we shouldn't bother you so early, but she's relentless!" Thomas said, laughing, a glint in his eye as he lovingly gazed at his wife.

"You're never a bother. Come in," Lorraine said, guiding them to the house. She was curious to see what might be inside the moving truck but didn't want to assume it was for her.

"See? I told you she'd be happy to see us," Mary Elle said, elbowing Thomas on his side.

"I'm sorry, there's nowhere for you to sit yet. Would you like some water?" Lorraine asked as she started pulling out a couple of Styrofoam cups.

"No, don't worry about us. We have a few things for you," Mary Elle said, unable to hide her excited smile.

Mary Elle's excitement was contagious, and Lorraine couldn't help but join in on her giddiness. "What is it?" she asked, eyes wide with excitement.

Before Mary Elle, and Thomas could answer, David and Cade brought various pieces of furniture into the home.

"What's all this?" Lorraine asked.

"I know your primary concern was getting Wyatt's room ready for him, and you had little money left over for anything else. So, your friend Lily came to us wanting to help. The town loves you, and we're all so proud of you. We got a few pieces together for you," Mary Elle said.

Lorraine was speechless. In the past, she would've hated to have anyone help her. She didn't like feeling like a charity case, but things were different now. No one was judging her or thinking she couldn't provide for Wyatt. They believed in her and wanted to make things easier for them.

"This means so much to me. Thank you," she said, hugging Mary Elle.

Lorraine wiped happy tears from her eyes as she pulled apart from Mary Elle.

"You're doing great things; if we can do anything to help, we will," Thomas said.

Lorraine nodded, unable to say anything, and gave Thomas a hug.

"Do you like this here?" David asked, motioning to a small round dining table with four chairs he had placed near the kitchen window right before the small pantry.

"It looks great there. Thank you," Lorraine said.

Her heart filled with joy as she saw her home coming together. For so many years, she had wished and prayed for a family. She had seen how others had a support system and had envied them. Lorraine wanted Wyatt to know what it was like to have aunts, uncles, grandparents, and cousins, but it had always been just the two of them for so long. Now they had more people supporting them than they could've ever imagined. Things might not have worked out how she had wanted them to, but they were better than she could've ever dreamed. Perhaps someday she could have a relationship with her parents and siblings, but if that never happened, they would be fine, too. They weren't alone anymore; they had a family and were part of an amazing community.

"What do you think?" Mary Elle asked, standing next to her now.

"I love it. I can't wait for Wyatt to see our home," Lorraine said, squeezing Mary Elle's hand.

It wasn't until this moment that Lorraine realized how much Mary Elle looked like her mother. She was beautiful. Mary Elle had lovely straight black hair that she kept neatly cut in a bob. She never let it get past her shoulders. Her eyes were bright blue and crinkled in the corners because she was always laughing and smiling.

"What's wrong?" Mary Elle asked.

"Nothing. I'm just so grateful to you and everyone. I don't know what I would do without y'all."

"Lorraine, you would do just fine without us because you are a strong, smart, hard-working woman. You don't need to do it alone anymore. You have all of us now," Mary Elle said, hugging her.

Once everyone was gone and she was alone again, Lorraine grabbed a blanket and book to sit outside. Her favorite thing about the house was probably the view of the mountains she had from the back deck. She imagined all the beautiful sunsets she would get to enjoy here. The breeze carried the sound of the birds singing and leaves rustling in the wind. She couldn't imagine being anywhere else but here.

She spent a few hours finishing her book. It was a regency romance, and she was having a hard time putting it down. Lorraine loved daydreaming about what life might've been like back then. What would she have looked like wearing all those beautiful gowns? She glanced at her watch and went back inside. Christian was coming over for dinner tonight, and she couldn't wait to see his reaction to the house being furnished.

Christian wasn't like any of the other men she had dated in the past. He was smart, charming, and very hardworking. He had recently finished his doctorate degree and gotten a position as a professor at the College. Christian encouraged her when she was feeling down and reminded her of her goals. Her friend Lily jokingly called them the power couple.

Lorraine had frozen lasagna and garlic bread thawing, and the oven was preheating. She hadn't had time to cook a homemade meal from scratch for Christian but figured he wouldn't mind the dinner she was preparing. The doorbell rang, and it was him.

"Hi," he said with a huge smile. He had bought her some roses and had a small box with him.

"Come in," Lorraine said as she kissed his cheek.

"Wow, the place looks great. You got furniture and everything," Christian said as he looked around. He was extremely proud of Lorraine's progress. He had tutored her in math and science during her first semester at college. Although studying wasn't Lorraine's strong suit, he knew she worked hard for Wyatt. She wanted to make him proud and show him she could improve herself and reach her goals as well.

"Yes, Mary Elle and Thomas surprised me today. The town got together and helped with the furniture and other things. I'm overjoyed. I wasn't expecting anything," Lorraine said as she stood beside him.

"Oh, here this is for you," he said as he handed the flowers and held out the small box for her to take.

"Thank you. These are beautiful," Lorraine said as she sniffed the flowers.

"This is for you too," he said as he took the flowers in his hands so Lorraine could grab the box from him.

"Oh, what is it?" she asked excitedly.

"Open it," he replied with a smile.

Lorraine opened the box to find a beautiful jade bonsai tree.

"It's so gorgeous. Thank you so much, Chris. I love it," Lorraine said, tears in her eyes.

"I got it for you. I know it will bring you good luck and positivity," Christian explained.

"I appreciate it. I was reading about them in a magazine lately," Lorraine added with a smile as she looked for the perfect spot to place her jade bonsai tree.

Soon dinner was ready, and they both sat down to eat dinner together.

"How is Wyatt?" Christian asked.

"He's doing well. He's at basketball practice with his friends. Their team has a game this Saturday. They are playing against Winding Creek High School," Lorraine said as she took a bite of the garlic bread.

"We should support him. Cheer him on and maybe go for lunch afterward," Christian said.

"He would love that," Lorraine replied.

Dinner was wonderful. Christian helped Lorraine clean up, and soon they cuddled on the sofa as they watched an episode of their favorite show about Vikings. Christian was just a couple of years older than Lorraine. He was a senior in high school when she was just a freshman. They had seen each other in town but had never interacted with each other until she started preparing herself to take the GED test. Mary Elle had hired Christian as Lorraine's private tutor to help her with the test. Then their friendship developed and now they were dating.

* * *

MARY ELLE and DeeAnn were enjoying a warm cup of tea when an incoming video call from Tiffany disrupted them.

"Hi, mom. We're in Atlanta now and will drive to Willow Heights soon," Tiffany said as she and David waited for their bags at the baggage claim area.

David chuckled, looking at her lovingly. "Tiffany has been counting down the minutes to see you guys."

"Good to hear from you guys. I can't wait to see you! Let me know when ya'll are on your way here. I'm at DeeAnn's," Mary Elle said, moving the phone so DeeAnn could come into view.

"Hi, Auntie Dee! We had the most amazing honeymoon in the Maldives. The beaches were beautiful, and the weather was perfect," Tiffany said.

David said, "We stayed in a villa with a private pool and beach area. It was like having our own paradise."

DeeAnn smiled, happy to see the newlyweds looking so in love. "That sounds wonderful! We can't wait to hear all about it."

They chatted for a few more minutes before ending the call.

"I was thinking about Sadie's first birthday," Mary Elle said. "I want to make her a book filled with pictures from her first year."

DeeAnn beamed with pride. "That's such a sweet idea. I can't wait to see it."

DeeAnn was sitting on a rocking chair holding her baby, Sadie. Mary Elle took a quick picture of the sweet moment.

"I can't believe that none of this would've ever happened if you hadn't reached out to me," DeeAnn said, glancing up at Mary Elle.

"Everything works out how it's meant to," Mary Elle said.

"I almost didn't respond to you. I was still angry and proud. If I hadn't set those feelings aside... I would've never moved here, met Paul, and given birth to this perfect baby girl."

"But you did, and now look at you. Living the life, you always wanted but didn't think you would ever have."

DeeAnn had lived in Willow Heights for a few years but was still in awe of its beauty. The mountains had a way of weaving themselves into your heart. Willow Heights was the perfect place for those looking to start over. Once here, you were filled with a sense of peace that is hard to find anywhere else. DeeAnn couldn't imagine living anywhere else. As she glanced at Mary Elle, she was overcome with emotion.

She felt like she'd been here all her life, though it hadn't been very long. All those years when she'd struggled with depression and loneliness seemed like such a distant memory. Everything she wanted and everything she needed, she had here. To think all of this was possible because she'd finally let go of the fear of rejection she'd felt inside. She'd finally let go of the negative thoughts that had plagued her.

When she was at her lowest, she took a leap, visited Mary Elle here, and fell in love with the small town. DeeAnn couldn't imagine a life without her family and friends in Willow Heights.

She looked out the window and saw a few deer grazing in the backyard. Paul lined their backyard with corn for the deer every morning before heading to work. The mountain views never got old, and DeeAnn loved the sound of the birds outside her window. She would always be grateful that she hadn't let her fears hold her back. That was a lesson she would be sure to instill in Sadie as well. The best things in life are always waiting for you on the other side of your fears.

CHAPTER 2

As soon as Patricia stepped out of her car, she could hear the faint sound of a baby crying. As she approached the front door, she could make out the sound of three kids crying. She took a deep breath and knocked on the front door.

Melanie flung the door open, and her face lit up at the sight of Patricia. "Patty! What a surprise, come in," she said, adjusting Harper in her arms.

"I bumped into Cade earlier, and he said you might like some company," Patricia said as she walked into the house, taking in the chaos of toys scattered on the floor. She smiled at Ryder, who was sitting on the floor, tears streaming down his face.

Sitting across from him on the floor, she said, "Hey Buddy, Auntie Patty is here to play with you."

Ryder's face brightened, and he quickly wiped away his tears. Patricia grabbed the firefighter truck he'd been playing with, and they played, with Patricia making silly faces and telling jokes to keep him entertained.

"Do you want me to hold Harper so you can get Hunter?" Patricia asked, extending her arms out.

"Yes, please. I am so sorry. Ryder woke up with a fever, and the twins are teething," Melanie said.

Patricia could see Melanie was trying her hardest to keep it together, but she could see the exhaustion in her eyes.

"You don't need to apologize. I can't imagine how hard it must be to juggle so much. How do you do it?"

Melanie laughed, "I don't know. Most days, I wake up and hope for the best."

Patricia watched as Melanie sat on the sofa with Hunter and soothed him. She felt an overwhelming sense of loss at the thought that she might never get to experience something like this. For as long as she could remember, she wanted to be a mother, but things hadn't worked out that way for her.

"What's wrong?" Melanie asked, noticing the somber look on her face.

Patricia tried to muster up a smile before answering, "It's silly," she said, shaking her head.

"Is it Dean?" Melanie asked.

"No, I haven't seen him since New Year."

"Really? I see him around town all the time," Melanie said.

"I've been avoiding him."

"I'm sorry things didn't work out between you two. I was really rooting for you," Melanie said as she rocked Hunter back and forth.

Patricia longed for that feeling, that kind of unconditional love between a mother and child, but it might never be in the cards for her.

"Are you dating?" Melanie asked.

"No, I haven't met anyone I like, but I have a date coming up with Anderson, Jasper's cousin."

"Oh, that's right! Britney told me about that. I can't wait

to hear all about it," Melanie said, smiling, but Patricia could see the fatigue in her friend's eyes.

"We'll see. Have you eaten today?" Patricia asked, feeling her own stomach grumble.

"No, and I haven't even showered since Friday."

"Oh, that's the smell," Patricia said jokingly.

"Hilarious," Melanie said.

"Now that the twins are asleep. Why don't you set them down, go shower, and I'll watch Ryder and prepare something for us to eat?" Patricia said.

"Are you sure you don't mind?" Melanie asked.

"Of course not. Go ahead!" Patricia said, waving her away.

Melanie took Hunter to the nursery, then returned to Harper.

"You're God-sent," Melanie said as she walked to the bathroom.

"Do you want to help me cook?" Patricia asked Ryder.

"Yes!" Ryder said excitedly.

Patricia grabbed the wooden step stool Thomas built for Ryder to help in the kitchen.

"The first order of business is washing our hands," Patricia said as she lathered Ryder's small hands with soap. Once they finished washing their hands, Ryder pointed at the aprons hanging on the wall, and Patricia put one on him and grabbed one for herself.

"Now we look like professionals," she said, which made Ryder giggle.

"Spaghetti?" Ryder said.

"Spaghetti sounds like a great idea! Let's see what we find," Patricia said as she began looking through the cabinets and refrigerator, grabbing all the ingredients.

Ryder helped her measure out the ingredients and stir the sauce. They laughed and joked as they worked. Patricia had so much fun cooking with Ryder that she didn't even notice when Melanie rejoined them.

"Mama!" Ryder said when he spotted her.

"It smells so good in here, Ryder!" Melanie said.

"Patty is a chef," Ryder said.

Finally, the meal was ready, and they gathered around the table to eat. The spaghetti was delicious, and Ryder beamed with pride as he told Melanie what he had helped make their meal. As they finished eating, Patricia offered to help clean up.

"Thanks for coming over and making dinner," Melanie said as they washed the dishes.

"I had a great time. Thanks for having me. We should do this more often," Patricia said.

"You're welcome here anytime."

As they said their goodbyes, Ryder ran up to Patricia and hugged her. "Thank you, Aunt Patty."

Patricia hugged him back, feeling a warmth in her chest that she hadn't felt in a long time. As she walked back to her car, she couldn't help but feel grateful for the opportunity to be a part of Melanie's family, even if it was just for a little while.

TIFFANY AND DAVID entered their home as husband and wife for the first time. Tiffany couldn't help the excited butterflies she felt in her stomach. They were both beaming with joy after an unforgettable honeymoon that had been filled with excitement, adventure, relaxation, and plenty of romance. As she walked around their barndominium, her mind rushed with possibilities. She couldn't wait to decorate and make memories here. The bare walls were calling to be filled with pictures of all their most cherished memories. Tiffany could already imagine their future kids running around and playing hide and seek. A broad smile spread across her face as David turned to face her with an equally bright smile on his face.

"Welcome to *our* home, Mrs. Clarke," David said as he turned to Tiffany and kissed her softly.

"Thank you, Mr. Clarke. I love the sound of that," Tiffany said, giggling.

"Well, there's a ton of boxes to unpack," David said as he looked around the living room area, knowing more boxes in the bedroom and garage needed to be sorted and unpacked.

"Oh, we didn't think of getting groceries," Tiffany sighed.

"It's ok. We can order in tonight. We are both jetlagged. We can go shopping tomorrow," David said as he looked at the drawer with the menus for their local restaurants.

"Sounds good. At least we have the sofa and bedroom furniture ready," Tiffany said as she headed to the bedroom where David had placed their luggage.

"Is Mary Elle coming over tonight?" David asked before calling to place an order from their favorite Mexican restaurant.

"Yes, she said she'd stop by after we have settled in," Tiffany replied, changing into comfortable lounging clothes.

Tiffany joined David in the living room. He was already moving the boxes from the garage into the living room. She helped him unpack. They were both eager to decorate their home and make it their own.

They had made a small dent with the moving boxes when there was a knock on the front door.

"Hi, yall, come on in!" Tiffany said as she hugged Mary Elle, and Thomas.

"You look gorgeous, sweetie! You have an amazing tan and look so relaxed. Tell me everything about your trip," Mary Elle said as she hugged Tiffany again.

"Maldives was amazing. We enjoyed it so much, and everything was beautiful. We met another couple on their honeymoon and became friends," Tiffany gushed as David joined them.

"David, you look great," Thomas said with a smile as he handed David some bags.

"What's this?" David asked as he tried to look into the bags.

"It's some groceries. We knew you wouldn't have time to go shopping, so we got some essentials," Thomas replied.

"You guys are amazing, thank you," David replied, heading to the kitchen to put the groceries away.

"Mom, Thomas, thank you so much," Tiffany said, smiling. She bent down and picked up her small dog. "Oh, my Livy bear! I've missed you, baby."

The small dog wagged her tail excitedly and licked Tiffany's face.

"You're welcome. Livy missed you guys so much. We wanted to make your transition into your home a little easier, especially after a long flight back home. I know you guys need to rest, and the jetlag must be horrible. We just came to drop that off for y'all," Mary Elle said.

"Thanks for dog-sitting for us. Don't worry. We just ordered some Mexican food thinking of you guys," Tiffany said as she led Mary Elle, and Thomas to their living room area.

"Oh, honey. You shouldn't have," Mary Elle said.

"Here, let me help you with some of these boxes," Thomas said as he saw David had unpacked more boxes.

"Food is here," David said as he approached the door.

The group gathered around the dining table to eat. The newlyweds shared photos they took during their honeymoon. Thomas and Mary Elle listened with delight as David and Tiffany recounted their favorite moments from the honeymoon. As the night drew to a close, a look of contentment was visible on all their faces.

"Thank you for having us over and for the lovely meal," Mary Elle said as she squeezed Tiffany's shoulder.

"Thanks for everything," David said, trying to keep himself from yawning.

"Don't worry about it. Get some rest," Thomas said as they said their goodbyes.

As soon as Mary Elle and Thomas left, they collapsed onto their bed, hugging each other. They were exhausted but happy.

"It's crazy to think this is just the beginning," David murmured, kissing the top of her head.

"What do you mean?" Tiffany asked, adjusting herself to look at him.

"This is the beginning of our life together, and I can't wait for what our future brings."

Tiffany smiled as she rested her head on his chest. She could hear his heart softly beating, and they were soon fast asleep.

CHAPTER 3

*D*eeAnn sat on the rocking chair in the nursery, cradling Sadie while waiting to talk to Sheila on the phone. She was excited to introduce Sadie to Sheila and their father but also nervous. She positioned her tablet on the dresser beside her and the video called Sheila.

"Hi Sheila, how are you and Dad?" DeeAnn asked as Sheila answered her call.

"We are great. Dad just had his routine checkup. He's healthy. Is that my beautiful niece?" Sheila asked.

"That's good to hear. Yes, this is little Sadie," DeeAnn said as she moved Sadie closer to the camera.

Sheila listened intently and cooed over every detail DeeAnn shared about Sadie. DeeAnn described every little detail about Sadie, from her curly hair to the sounds she made while asleep.

"I can't wait to meet her," Sheila said.

"I wanted to know if I could come to visit this week with Sadie and Paul?" DeeAnn asked.

"That's a great idea! Dad's been asking about you all day," Sheila replied.

"Great. I think we'll be able to go tomorrow. I want Dad to meet Sadie before he completely forgets me," DeeAnn said with a sad smile.

"I know. I understand. It's difficult to see his memory decline," Sheila said.

Sheila filled her in on their father's condition and how difficult it was to watch him struggle with his memory and everyday tasks. DeeAnn felt a small wave of sadness come over her, and she thought about how their father might not recognize them at all soon. Sadie might never have a relationship with him, and her heart sank at that thought. DeeAnn noticed the somber look on Sheila's face. She couldn't imagine how difficult it must be for Sheila to see Gregory's health decline and how Alzheimer's affected him.

"Even if he doesn't recognize us, he will always be able to feel the love and warmth of being surrounded by family," Sheila said as if reading DeeAnn's thoughts.

"How are you doing, Sheila?" DeeAnn asked gently.

"It's hard. It's hard to see him struggling with things that were so easy for him before. Sometimes he gets upset with himself because he can't remember things. I wish there were more we could do to help him. Sometimes I feel like I'm losing him more and more each day..."

"Yes, I can't imagine how hard this is on you, too. It must be so hard to see him going through this. Maybe we should look into a support group for caregivers?" DeeAnn suggested.

"I really like that idea. Sometimes I feel like this is too much for me to handle," Sheila said.

"Take care of yourself, too. It's okay to ask for help. I don't want you to burn yourself out. We will get through this. I am here for you and will try to make more of an effort," DeeAnn said.

"Thanks, Dee. I can't wait to see you and your little family tomorrow."

The sisters said their goodbyes, and DeeAnn sat silently for a few minutes. She wished there was more that she could do to take the load off of Sheila.

* * *

Lorraine sat outside on her front porch, waiting for Wyatt to come over. She noticed Mrs. Adelman coming her way down the street, and, for a second, she considered going back inside her house. She knew Mrs. Adelman meant well, but it was no secret that anything you told her would soon make it around town.

"Hello there, Lorraine! Nice place," Mrs. Adelman said, letting out a small whistle.

"Thank you. I love it so much," Lorraine said with a broad smile as Mrs. Adelman approached her.

"It's been so good to see you getting back on your feet. I always believed in you," Mrs. Adelman said.

"Thank you. I feel like I'm in a good place right now."

"A little birdie also told me there's a new man in your life," the older woman said with a mischievous smile.

Lorraine laughed and felt a blush creeping onto her cheeks. "Yes. He's an amazing man. He treats me well and is a total gentleman. He's great with Wyatt too."

Mrs. Adelman leaned in and said, "Well, I am just so thrilled for you. You deserve all the happiness. Everyone says I'm the town gossip, but I only love and care for everyone in this community. I've seen you grow up here, and I've seen your struggles. If anyone deserves to have someone who loves and supports them, it's you."

"Thank you, Mrs. Adelman. I truly am happy right now."

Mrs. Adelman patted her hand. "Now do tell, who is the lucky gent?"

Lorraine laughed. "We're keeping it private for now."

"Sounds like a good idea. Enjoy this new chapter in your life and soak up every second. You deserve to be happy, my dear!"

The ladies hugged and said their goodbyes. Lorraine smiled as she watched Mrs. Adelman walk away. It felt good to know that she had people that were rooting for her happiness. Just then, she saw Wyatt jogging down the street with an excited smile.

"Hey, mom! I've got some good news."

"Hi baby, what's going on?

"Coach told me there will be scouts at our game next month!" Wyatt said. His excitement was too much for him to stand still.

"That's amazing! I am sure you will blow them away."

Wyatt sat next to Lorraine on the steps. "I hope so. My grades are good, but not good enough to get me any scholarships."

"My grandmother would always say that what's meant for you, nothing can take away," Lorraine said, bumping her shoulder to his.

"Are you excited about our hiking trip this weekend?"

"I sure am. I'm thinking of making your favorite sandwich to take on the trip. The one with the creamed cheese and apples with arugula."

"Oh, yum! Can I have one now?" Wyatt asked, standing up.

Lorraine quickly stood, happy to see his excitement over the sandwich. "Of course! Let's go inside."

Wyatt sat at the dining table as Lorraine pulled out the ingredients from the fridge.

Lorraine placed the sandwiches on the table and sat across from Wyatt. "I'm a little nervous about this weekend."

"Why?" Wyatt asked before taking a bite of his sandwich.

She shrugged and sighed. "I want you and Christian to get along."

"We do. He's a cool guy."

Lorraine nodded. She wished she could adopt Wyatt and Christian's laid-back and easygoing attitude. Instead, she was always overthinking and expecting the worst.

"Hey, Mom?" Wyatt said.

"Yeah?" Lorraine asked, turning to face him.

"Thanks for everything you do," Wyatt said and hugged her.

* * *

As she walks down the path that leads to the fountain on the main square, Patricia takes a deep breath and tries to calm her nerves. She had never been set up on a blind date but knew it was time to put herself back out there. This was her first date in a very long time. They had agreed to meet at the mini golf course near the main square. As she arrived, she saw Anderson waiting for her by the entrance. Anderson walks towards her, looking handsome and confident in a plaid shirt and jeans. "Hey Patty!" he calls out, flashing her a dazzling smile. "You look beautiful tonight."

Patricia feels her cheeks turn red as she smiles back at him. "Oh, this old thing?" she says, running her hands down the front of her floral dress. "Thank you, Anderson. You look great too."

They made small talk as they walked to the mini golf course.

"I hope you're ready for a challenging game of mini golf!" Patricia says.

The course was on the outskirts of town, surrounded by lush trees and towering mountains in the distance.

As they made their way to the first hole, Anderson told Patricia about his most recent trip, and she shared stories about her love for hiking and exploring the outdoors.

They spent the next hour playing mini-golf and laughing at each other as they tried to hit the ball into the holes. As they played, they laughed and joked with each other, trying to outdo one another with their putting skills. Patricia relaxed in Anderson's company. He was easy to talk to and had a great sense of humor. Anderson was a good sport, even when she accidentally hit him with her putter. They bonded over their shared interests, and she forgot that this was technically a blind date. Although they'd seen photos of each other before coming out, they'd never spoken before.

"Great job, Patty!" Anderson exclaimed as she sunk her ball into a hole.

"Thanks," she replied, grinning at him.

They continued playing; they felt a connection and enjoyed each other's company. Anderson turned to her as they made their way to the last hole. "I hope you've had a good time. Usually, blind dates are a miss, but I've really enjoyed getting to know you."

Patricia smiled. "I've had a lot of fun today as well, Anderson."

Anderson surprised her by saying, "I think this is the best first date I've ever had."

Patricia smiled at him. "I'm so glad to hear that. I'm having a great time, too."

As they finished their game, Patricia couldn't help but feel grateful that Britney and Jasper had convinced her to go on this date. She did not know where things would go with Anderson, but she was excited to find out.

CHAPTER 4

It had been six wonderful months of maternity leave for Melanie, filled with countless memories of her three beautiful kids. Despite the challenges she faced caring for three kids under the age of four, Melanie handled it with grace and gratitude for the strength that God gave her to continue being a good wife and mother. Though Melanie never complained, Cade, her husband, knew she felt overwhelmed and lonely. Cade tried to help her as much as he could.

As Melanie was cutting up some apples for Ryder, Cade approached her and hugged her. "Are you ready to return to Willow Acres?" he asked.

Melanie looked over at Harper and Hunter, who were playing in their playpen. "Yes, I'm excited but also nervous about leaving the kids at the daycare," she replied.

"Don't worry. They'll be fine. Besides, they'll have their big brother to look out for them," Cade reassured her as he helped her serve their dinner.

Melanie expressed her concerns about the daycare, but

Cade reminded her of the positive things she had heard from other moms in town and their visit to the daycare.

"Very true. I've spoken with several other moms in town, and they all rave about Ms. Eckerson and her daycare. They are now offering pre-k for the bigger kids. I've also met with her and visited the daycare already; it seemed very nice," Melanie replied as she got some iced tea from the fridge for Cade.

As they enjoyed their meal together, Cade expressed his gratitude for all that Melanie does for their family. "Thanks, honey. I know I don't say this enough, but thank you for all you do for us," Cade said as he squeezed her hand.

Melanie smiled and replied, "I try to do my best. I love our little family so much."

Cade suggested they invite Tiffany and David to go to the lake with them over the weekend now that they're back from their honeymoon. Melanie quickly agreed but realized that she hadn't had the chance to contact Tiffany yet. She grabbed her phone and texted her, but Cade wondered if it was too late.

"Yeah, she must be tired. It was a long journey to and from there," Melanie said, knowing how exhausting long flights can be.

Cade reassured her, "Don't worry, honey. I'm sure you'll have time to catch up soon."

Melanie couldn't help but wish that she and Cade could escape to a beautiful place like the Maldives and have their own little paradise. But for now, she was content with the love and happiness surrounding her at home.

* * *

Lorraine woke up extra early on Saturday morning to prepare sandwiches, water, and other snacks for the hiking trip. She had taken a melatonin gummy the night before, hoping to get a good night's sleep to wake up feeling refreshed, but she'd spent the night tossing and turning. She was falling for Christian fast and hard, and she worried she might go too fast.

Lorraine didn't have the best track record for making great decisions in her relationships with men, which kept her up at night. She loved Wyatt so much and wanted to prove to him and everyone that she could be a great mother. Lorraine knew Wyatt worried about her, and she hated that because of her. He couldn't be like any other teen. He constantly checked on her, and she knew that even if he didn't voice his concerns, he worried she might go down the wrong path again.

As she approached Wyatt's bedroom door, she took a deep breath. She opened the door and watched as he lay in bed peacefully sleeping. The soft glow of the sun rising was the only light illuminating the room. Lorraine can't help but smile as she watched him. An overwhelming sense of love and protection washed over her. Memories of his early years flood her mind. All those sleepless nights when she was scared of what the future held for them.

All those nights when it was just the two of them. Memories of the first time he said mom and his first steps. They'll never have those moments again, but they could make new memories. She knew there might be some hard times up ahead, but she was confident they could get through anything together. Wyatt stirred in his sleep, bringing her back to the present moment.

Lorraine gently shook him. "It's time to wake up, honey."

Wyatt rubbed his eyes and slowly sat up. "Is there breakfast?"

"I'll make you an egg, bacon, and cheese sandwich. Hurry, Chris is almost here." Lorraine walked to the kitchen to make

Wyatt's sandwich and ensure she hadn't forgotten to pack anything.

Just as Lorraine finished making the breakfast sandwiches, there was a knock on the front door. Lorraine felt her heart speed up.

"It must be Christian."

Christian stood at the front door with a wide smile on his face. "Good morning, beautiful. Are you guys ready?"

Lorraine gave him a quick kiss on the lips. "I made you some breakfast, and then we can go."

Christian followed Lorraine inside and said hello to Wyatt.

"Hey, Chris," Wyatt said in between bites.

Christian sat across from Wyatt, and they quickly delved into their plans for the day.

"This is for you. Would you like some orange juice?" Lorraine asked.

"No, but I wouldn't mind a nice cup of Joe," Christian said as he took a mug and poured himself black coffee.

"Cream and sugar?" Lorraine offered.

"Sure. I will have some sugar, please," Christian replied.

"Here you go," Lorraine said as she got the sugar and a spoon out for Christian.

"Are we going to fish today?" Wyatt asked with a smile. He loved being in nature and mentioned several times that he wanted to go fishing.

"Yes, we can fish. I brought three fishing rods with me," Christian said as he rejoined Wyatt at the kitchen counter.

"That's awesome. I've been asking Mom, Mary Elle, and Thomas to go fishing, but everyone's been so busy lately," Wyatt explained.

"You got it, buddy. We'll do the hike, and there's a lake at the trail's end. My dad and I went fishing there all the time and caught some snappers. Next time, we should camp for at least one night there. You can see stars, and the air is fresh and clean up there. You would love it," Chris said excitedly.

Seeing Christian and Wyatt interacting this way made Lorraine's heart melt. She knew Christian was being genuine and enjoyed spending time with Wyatt. Christian was everything she had ever wanted as a father figure for Wyatt.

"Lunch, snacks, and drinks are all packed," Lorraine announced.

Christian finished the last of his coffee. "I'll start loading them into the truck."

Lorraine and Christian had both planned this trip with the purpose of bonding with Wyatt. Christian wanted to show Lorraine he was serious about their relationship. They both had worked hard to keep their relationship a secret at the college but wanted to spend time together.

* * *

When DeeAnn, Paul, and Sadie arrived at Gregory's house, Sheila warmly welcomed them. She smiled and expressed her happiness to see them all.

"I've missed you!" DeeAnn said, hugging her sister.

"Me too. Is that my precious niece?" Sheila asked.

"This is Sadie," Paul said as he handed Sadie to Sheila to carry her for the first time. Sadie was now three weeks old.

"Here, let me take a photograph," DeeAnn said as she pulled out her cell phone to capture when Sheila met Sadie. Sheila was delighted to pose for the camera, her smile wide and eyes shining.

"You're so silly," Sheila said as she smiled at the camera.

DeeAnn asked about their dad, and Sheila informed her he was inside, sitting on his rocking chair, lost in thought. DeeAnn approached him, feeling both nervous and excited. She gently touched his shoulder to bring him back to reality.

"Dad," DeeAnn said softly.

"DeeAnn, it's so good to see you," Gregory said as he smiled at her.

"Dad, I want you to meet your granddaughter, Sadie," DeeAnn said as Sheila brought Sadie to him.

When DeeAnn introduced Sadie, Gregory's eyes lit up with joy. "She's beautiful. She looks so much like you, DeeAnn," he said, his voice choked with emotion.

DeeAnn asked if he wanted to hold Sadie, and he nodded eagerly. Paul took several photos and videos, ensuring they always had this special memory captured on film.

As they sat and chatted, Gregory shared stories of DeeAnn and Sheila's childhood, which made them all laugh. Although Gregory and DeeAnn hadn't reconnected until recently, he had been a part of her life for the first few years. They looked through old photo albums, which triggered more memories and laughter. The day passed quickly, and DeeAnn was glad to see her father so happy and engaged.

Before leaving, DeeAnn hugged her father tightly and whispered, "I love you, Dad." He whispered back, "Thank you for letting me meet Sadie. I love you both very much." DeeAnn knew her father might not remember this moment for long, but she would cherish it forever in her heart.

As they said their goodbyes, DeeAnn promised to come and visit again soon. They walked out of the house with smiles on their faces, grateful for the special time they had spent with family.

CHAPTER 5

Patricia felt her hands getting sweaty as she waited for the rest of the ladies to show up. They celebrated Melanie's return to work and agreed to meet at the main square. She glanced at her watch again and wished she had stayed in her car. The last thing she wanted was to run into Dean. She hated she felt so out of place in her own town. Sometimes she wished she had never dated Dean, but then she remembers their relationship and the memories they shared, and she wouldn't take it back. No matter how painful they were now, she knew she would look back at them sometime down the road and smile.

Patricia felt her stomach drop when she spotted him. He hadn't seen her yet, but she knew it was only a matter of time. She stood frozen in place, unsure of what to do.

"Patty?"

She tried to muster up a smile but felt like she might throw up. "Hi."

"What are you doing here?"

"I'm waiting for someone."

Dean's face fell as if he had suddenly remembered a very sad memory. "Oh, you have a date?"

She immediately considered lying to him, but this was a small town, and he would know she lied in no time.

"The girls and I are meeting up for lunch. We're celebrating that Melanie is going back to work."

"That's neat. Do you have plans for tomorrow?"

"Yes," she lied.

"I'd like to have a moment with you. Catch up and all that."

Patricia wanted to say yes. Her brain and heart were yelling at her to say yes, but she remembered how sad she'd been when they broke up. She was heartbroken when she heard her coworker Christina talking about her dates with Dean, and she wasn't ready to put herself out there again.

"I'm very busy with work."

A sad smile spread across his face, and Patricia almost reached out to hug him, but she held herself back.

"I understand."

"Hey! I was looking for you," Tiffany said, appearing out of nowhere.

Patricia smiled, grateful for the distraction. "Hi! Is anyone else here?"

"No, not yet. Maybe we can wait for them outside the steakhouse? Hi, Dean!"

"Hey, Tiff. Enjoy your day, ladies. If you want a sweet treat, pass by the food truck afterward. We have churros."

"Sure thing. Sounds good," Tiffany said.

Tiffany turned to Patricia once Dean was gone.

"Thanks for saving me."

"Are you okay?"

Patricia sighed as they fell into step and walked toward Papaw's steakhouse. "Yeah, I'm fine. This happens when you live in a small town. You bump into your ex everywhere you go."

"Ugh, sounds horrible. I'm sorry." Tiffany leaned down to pet a cat sitting outside the restaurant.

"Is it lost?"

"No, David told me he's Paw's cat. He comes with him to work every day. He waits outside all day, entertaining guests, then walks home with Paw every night after the restaurant closes."

Soon, Sienna and Melanie joined them. It felt good to be out with friends. She had missed this. For the first time in a long time, she wasn't stuck at home wallowing in self-pity. Maybe it was time to put herself out there again. She was too young to turn into a hermit. There was a lot that she still had to do and see. What would her grandma Ann say if she knew she had let a breakup stop her from living her life? Grandma Ann had always been courageous and a daredevil. She had instilled in Patricia the belief that she could do anything she set her mind to. She didn't need to ask anyone for permission. We only got one life, and we had to make it count. Patricia was done holding herself back. Sitting here with a strong group of women who loved and encouraged her was all she needed to get back in the saddle.

Melanie arrived at the office early, excited to see all her coworkers and get back to work after her maternity leave. Since she was off today, Cade had taken the kids to Tiffany's house since she volunteered to babysit. Melanie walked in with a smile on her face. She had been away for months on maternity leave, and while she loved spending time with her kids, she was excited to be back at work. Bailey from accounting greeted her while munching on a blueberry muffin.

"Hey, Melanie! Welcome back. I missed you!" Bailey exclaimed, her mouth full of the muffin.

Melanie laughed and hugged her. "Thanks, Bailey! It's good to be back. I missed you too!"

As she made her way to her office, Lisa from the bakery, stopped her with a matcha latte.

"Welcome back, Mel! I hope this latte helps you get through the day," Lisa said with a smile.

Melanie thanked her and sipped the latte before continuing to her office. She felt a pang of sadness in her chest as she thought about her kids. She missed them terribly, but she knew they were in good hands. As she sat down at her desk, Mary Elle walked in, checking in to see how her first day back was going.

"Hi, Mom! It's going great so far. It feels good to be back."

"That's wonderful to hear, sweetheart. Let me know if you need anything."

As Mary Elle left for her office, Melanie noticed a delivery man walking towards her with a bouquet of beautiful flowers.

"Melanie?" the deliveryman asked.

"That's me!" she said.

He handed her the bouquet. "These are for you," he said. "Please sign here."

Melanie placed the flowers on her desk, then signed off that she received them. The card attached read, "I love you. Have a great first day back. Love always, Cade."

Melanie smiled as she sniffed the flowers. Her heart swelled with love for her husband. She quickly sent him a text message to thank him for the flowers. She placed a photograph of her small family on her desk to glance at every time she missed them.

As lunchtime approached, Melanie called Tiffany to check in on the kids.

"Hey, Tiff! How's everything going?"

"The kids are doing great. We went for a walk earlier, and now they're napping. How's your first day back?" Tiffany asked.

"It's been wonderful so far. Everyone has been kind, and I'm thankful to be back."

"That's great. Harper just woke up. I'll see you later."

Melanie hung up the phone and noticed Thomas walking into her office. She smiled as he approached. She could smell the scent of freshly baked cookies as he walked in.

"Hey, Melanie! I brought you some fresh cookies from the bakery," Thomas said, holding out the box of cookies.

"Thank you so much, Thomas! You didn't have to do that," Melanie said, touched by his gesture. Thomas was such a good boss and husband to her mother.

"It's no big deal. I wanted to make your first day back a little sweeter."

Melanie smiled, feeling grateful for Thomas. He was a great, supportive boss. She couldn't dream of a better workplace.

"If you want to leave early today, it's fine with me. I know you miss the kids," Thomas said.

Melanie thought for a moment before replying, "Thank you for the offer, Thomas. But I think I'll stay until 4 pm. I want to get back into the rhythm and finish everything before I go home."

Thomas nodded in understanding, "Alright. Sounds good. If you need anything, let me know."

*   *   *

After a few hours of hiking, Lorraine, Christian, and Wyatt arrived at a beautiful waterfall. They sat on some rocks and enjoyed the scenery and the calming sound of the water. The trail had been steep and rocky, but they'd had a good time.

Christian and Wyatt spread a blanket, and Lorraine pulled out their sandwiches.

"I can't believe I've never been here before," Lorraine said.

Wyatt reached out and grabbed a sandwich and some chips. "Thanks for bringing us, Chris. It's nice to get away."

Lorraine and Christian shared a smile. "We should do this more often. What do you say? Once a month, at least?"

Wyatt nodded excitedly. "Sounds good to me."

They ate their sandwiches, and Christian shared random facts he knew about the trees, plants, and animals they had seen on their hike. It all completely fascinated Wyatt and Lorraine was beaming seeing the two getting along so well.

They removed their shoes and socks and dipped their feet in the water to cool off. Lorraine felt Christian watching her, and she turned to face him. They shared a smile, and he took her hand in his. Lorraine smiled, feeling grateful for this moment and for his company. Christian and Wyatt jumped into the water, splashing, laughing, and having fun. Lorraine watched with glee and took pictures and videos of them.

After they dried off and put their shoes back on, they gathered their things and continued the hike. The higher they climbed, the more beautiful the view became. Lorraine was glad that they'd come on this hike. She wasn't the most outdoorsy person but was having a good time.

"How are you doing back there?" Christian asked, turning to face her.

Lorraine wiped the sweat off her forehead. "I'm good!"

"Wow, this is so beautiful!" Wyatt exclaimed, taking in the view.

"It truly is breathtaking," Christian said, putting an arm around Lorraine once she joined them at the top.

Lorraine let out a satisfied sigh. The view was amazing, but nothing could compare to how she felt inside. She couldn't stop smiling, watching Wyatt and Christian bonding. They were both grinning from ear to ear and snapping pictures on their cellphones. The cool air up here was refreshing, and the surrounding wilderness was like something out of a movie.

Lorraine's heart was full of satisfaction and love as they descended the trail. The day had gone better than she could've ever imagined. As they approached the area where they would go fishing, Wyatt dashed off and set everything up.

"This has been the best day ever!" he said.

"I'm glad you enjoyed it," Christian said.

"Thanks for bringing me, man. I hope we can do this more often."

"We will," Christian said and gave Lorraine a kiss on the cheek before heading toward the water with Wyatt.

As Lorraine lay down on the blanket with her book, she smiled as she heard Wyatt and Christian chatting. In her heart, she knew this was only the beginning of their wonderful life together.

CHAPTER 6

The sparkling gems greeted Mary Elle when she walked into Rita's store. Rita and Emma were busy arranging their new creations on the display shelves. Ever since Emma returned, she and Rita had bonded while making jewelry together. Mary Elle smiled as she approached them. She loved seeing how well things were going between Rita and Emma.

"Hey there, ladies," she said, her voice carrying a note of cheerfulness. "What's new?"

Rita looked up from the necklace's display. "We have some gorgeous new pieces. Come look," she said, holding up a necklace. "Isn't it stunning?"

"That is gorgeous!" Mary Elle said.

"We've been working hard to add new designs to our collection. I'm so grateful to create all these beautiful pieces with Rita. After everything that happened, I didn't think I'd have a second chance at making things right, but here I am. It's a blessing," Emma said.

Mary Elle couldn't help but feel a surge of happiness at Emma's words. She had known Emma and Rita since they were all kids and had watched as they struggled through some tough times. Emma had been through a lot in her personal life, but she had taken responsibility for her actions and worked hard to turn her life around.

"It's amazing how life blesses us with second chances," Mary Elle mused aloud. "Everyone deserves a chance to make things right."

"We can finish this tomorrow. Are you all ready for dinner? We could order Chinese?" Rita said.

"Yes! I'm starving," Emma said.

"You can never go wrong with Chinese," Mary Elle said.

As they drove up Rita's driveway, the ladies grew alarmed. A man exited the house, and when he saw them, he ran.

Rita and Mary Elle pulled out their cell phones to call the police, but Emma stopped them. "Please don't call the cops," she pleaded. "He's an old friend of mine. He's harmless."

Rita's face turned red with anger. "Emma, is this the same guy who broke into our house before?" she asked sternly.

Emma's eyes dropped to the ground as she confirmed it was the same person. Emma explained she left the door open for him to sneak inside when no one was home so that he could shower and eat. She had been ashamed of what they would think if they knew about him.

Rita shook her head in disbelief.

"Emma, you know better than this. You can't just let anyone into our home, and it's probably not good for you to still be associated with him when you're so new on your recovery journey."

Mary Elle placed a hand on Emma's shoulder. "We understand that you're trying to help him, but you can't put yourself and others in danger like this."

Emma nodded. "I'm sorry," she whispered. "I just didn't know what to do."

The ladies spent the rest of the evening talking to Emma and offering their support. They looked up shelters and programs that might help her friend. When Mary Elle left, Rita locked all the doors and watched for any signs of trouble. Despite the scare earlier that night, she was grateful that she finally had some answers, and she hoped they could help Emma's friend. The last thing she wanted was for her sister to feel helpless and relapse.

* * *

Cade surprised Melanie with a date night that he had spent weeks planning. This was their first date night since the twins were born, and they missed having dinner together and going on romantic walks by the lake. Melanie stood in front of the mirror, finishing her makeup, when she received a text.

"We are on our way," Tiffany said via text message.

"Great! See you soon," Melanie replied.

She rushed to the kitchen to leave some milk bottles ready for Harper and Hunter in case they got hungry while they were out. Ryder was in his highchair having his favorite dinner, spaghetti with meatballs, carrot pieces, and grapes.

"Cade, they are almost here. Are you ready?" Melanie asked him as she walked into their bedroom, where Cade had been getting ready.

"Almost done," Cade said as he looked up at Melanie and noticed her beauty. Melanie had done her hair into a nice half bun; her makeup was a gorgeous, effortless look with golden eyeshadow; she was wearing a knit short-sleeve dress in a light cream color with some ankle boots. Melanie also had a dark green cardigan in case it was chilly out. The couple had opted to have dinner at their favorite Italian place and would have dessert at Dean's truck.

"Do I look ok?" Melanie asked as she noticed Cade staring at her.

"Yes, you look beautiful," Cade said as he stood up and gave her a kiss on the lips. He fell in love with her more and more each day.

Melanie smiled. "Thank you. You look handsome, as always."

Even though she was excited to get some alone time with Cade, she couldn't help feeling nervous. She knew that David and Tiffany would take great care of the kids, but it never got easier to be away from them. As if sensing her unease, Cade pulled her into his arms. Melanie let out a deep breath and rested her head on his chest. She could hear his heart beating and let out a long sigh.

Cade raised her chin. "Everything is going to be okay. We deserve this night out."

The knock on the door reactivated all the nervous feelings in her stomach. Melanie stood back as Cade let Tiffany and David in.

"Hi guys, thanks for coming," Cade said as he greeted them.

David walked over to Ryder and gave him a high five. "No problem, we love taking care of the little rascals."

"Well, we'll be back soon," Melanie said as she grabbed her cardigan and purse.

"Have fun," Tiffany replied, smiling.

"We will," Melanie replied with a wink.

Tiffany and David sat on the sofa as they listened to the playful sounds the kids made. Tiffany loved being an aunt but couldn't wait to be a mother. She was most excited to see David with their kids.

"This is nice," Tiffany said.

David turned to look at her. "Great minds."

"You were thinking the same thing?"

David nodded before he walked over to Ryder.

"Ready to build the train tracks?" David asked Ryder, who had just finished his dinner.

The twins stretched their little arms toward Tiffany, asking to be let out of the playpen.

"Ok, let's go. You first, Hunter," Tiffany said as she picked him up and gave him a hug before placing him on the floor mat. The twins were now crawling and were faster.

"Hi there, buddy," David said as he greeted Hunter.

"Now it's your turn, pretty girl," Tiffany said as she grabbed Harper, who jumped up to meet her arms.

"Wow, you jumped high," Tiffany said as she hugged her tight before placing her on her lap as she sat down on the sofa across from David and the boys.

"Hello, Miss Harper," David said as he waved at her, which caused her to burst into a fit of giggles. The twins were friendly and loved to spend time with Tiffany and David.

"I can't wait to have our little family," Tiffany said as she watched David with the kids.

Tiffany didn't realize how much she yearned to be a mother until now. Spending time with the kids and David just stirred that longing inside her even more.

* * *

MELANIE AND CADE sat in a cozy corner of the restaurant. Melanie couldn't stop smiling as she looked across the table at Cade. She didn't know how she had gotten so lucky with him. She fell more in love with him every day. Cade walked into her life when she needed him the most. Raising kids with him was the best thing in the world. Seeing how he was as a father to their three kids made her heart happy. Cade never treated Ryder differently than how he treated the twins.

"How's your baked ziti?" Cade asked Melanie.

"It's fantastic. How's your chicken marsala?" Melanie asked Cade as she took a sip of the pinot noir.

"Excellent. Their garlic bread was amazing as well."

"I have missed having dinner out with you."

"Me too, darling," Cade said as she pulled a small box out of his pocket and placed it in front of Melanie.

"What's this?"

"It's a little something for you. I want you to know that I love you with all my heart. I'm beyond grateful that God answered my prayer, which was to allow me to be with you," Cade said as he leaned in and gave Melanie a kiss on the lips.

Melanie opened the box and found a lovely ring with an iridescent oval cut Napolean opal at the center, surrounded by six small white round-cut diamonds set on 14k gold.

Melanie removed the ring from the box to see how it looked on her. It fit her middle finger on her right hand perfectly. "Wow," she said, admiring the ring.

"Do you like it?" Cade asked, a little nervous.

Melanie looked down at her hand and admired the ring.

Cade let out a relieved sigh. "I'm glad you like it. It took Rita a few months to find that opal. I was nervous it wasn't to your liking."

"No, it's perfect," Melanie said with happy tears.

"I wanted you to know that I appreciate everything you do for us. I know it's been difficult, but I hope you always know how much I love and admire you."

"I wasn't expecting this. It was a wonderful surprise. Thank you. Believe it or not, no matter how difficult it's gotten for me lately, I couldn't have asked for a better family."

After dinner, Cade and Melanie walked down the main square, hand in hand. They walked over to Dean's food truck. It was chilly outside, so they got churros and some hot cocoa.

"Fancy seeing you guys past 7 pm," Dean said with a small laugh.

"We are on a date," Melanie said, smiling.

"Nice. How are the kids?" Dean asked.

"Good, at home with Tiffany and David," Cade replied.

"I heard you're back at Willow Acres?" Dean asked.

"Yup, back after six months off. I can't complain. It was nice being home with the kids, and it's also nice being back at work now."

"I ran into Patty a couple of days ago," Dean said with a sad smile.

"Are you ok?" Cade asked, confused by the look on Dean's face.

"I don't know. I guess I..." Dean said but didn't finish before being interrupted by another customer.

"We can talk later," Melanie offered before sitting at a table near the food truck.

Out of earshot, Cade said, "I wonder what's going on with him. I've never seen him like that before."

"Patty seemed pretty down the last time I saw her, too. Mom's convinced that they'll get back together."

"They were good together."

Suddenly, Dean approached their table.

"Sorry, guys. I've just been thinking a lot lately," Dean began, "but I don't know what to do."

"What's wrong?" Cade asked Dean.

"Well, ever since Patty and I broke up, things haven't been the same. I loved her and know we both were immature and said things we didn't mean and ended up breaking up, but now that I've dated a couple of women, I know I want to be back with her. She's the one I love, but she's not interested. Honestly, I can't blame her," Dean shared with them.

"Dean, you want to talk things through with her?" Cade asked, making sure he understood him clearly.

"Yes. It took me this long to figure out that I truly love her, and there's no other girl for me," Dean replied, glancing away with a sad look in his eyes.

"Ok, that's good. I think you need to have a talk with Patty," Melanie said, smiling. She knew Patty was still in love with Dean and would hear him out.

"I tried talking to her. I asked her if we could talk, and she was busy," Dean said, deflated.

"Dean, maybe when you asked her, she was busy, but that doesn't mean she doesn't want to speak with you ever again. I would encourage you to ask her again and see what she says," Melanie offered.

"You would do that?"

"Of course. I know you love her, and even though it was painful, I think the breakup was good for both of you."

"I never stopped loving her. I was just focused on getting the food truck to take off, and I couldn't put as much effort into our relationship."

Cade put his hand on Dean's shoulder. "Talk things out. You lose nothing by letting her know how you feel."

"Yeah, I guess I just felt like she wasn't interested in hearing me out. I will try again," Dean said with a hopeful smile. It was just a matter of time before they ran into each other again.

CHAPTER 7

*A*fter a long day of exams, all Lorraine wanted was some peace. She still had one more midterm to do today, and then she would be free. She couldn't wait to get home and binge-watch some of her favorite television shows. School had been really kicking her butt lately, and she felt like she was struggling, which worried her. If she didn't keep her grades up, she wouldn't be able to get into the nursing program. Lorraine didn't even want to think about what she would do if she didn't get into the program.

"I thought I might find you here," Christian said, sitting across from her on the picnic table.

Lorraine looked around nervously. "Taking a break between classes."

"How are your exams going?"

Lorraine sighed. "My brain hurts. I keep thinking about what I'll do if I don't get into the nursing program."

Christian covered her hands with his. "Don't even think about that. It's not an option. You've worked hard. I've seen your grades, and you're right on track."

Lorraine smiled and quickly removed her hands away from his while glancing around nervously.

"What's wrong?" Christian asked.

"It's silly, but I don't want anyone to see us together."

"Why?"

Lorraine shrugged. "Small town and people talk."

"We're not doing anything wrong, but I understand. I'll see you later, okay?"

She watched him go toward his office. Christian made her the happiest she had ever been. She felt safe in their relationship, but she didn't want anyone to think he was the reason she got into the program.

"Are you ready for the test?" Jade asked, sliding into where Christian had just been sitting.

"I sure hope so!" Lorraine said and laughed. She liked Jade. She was younger than Lorraine by five years, but they got along well and often studied together.

"I've been so nervous that I haven't eaten all day, and now I'm starving."

Lorraine dug through her purse. "I have a granola bar if you want it."

"Yes, please! You're a lifesaver."

"I can grab us something to drink from the vending machine if you'd like?"

"No, I have my water bottle. Thanks," Jade said.

They took their notecards out and began to study. Jade was the only person who understood the kind of stress and pressure Lorraine was under. Lorraine felt lucky to have Jade as a friend.

Her thoughts turned to Christian. They had been seeing each other for a few months now, and she dreaded what might happen if any of her classmates knew she was dating a professor. Although Christian wasn't one of their professors, she didn't want anyone to think she got special treatment.

Lorraine sighed and shook her head, trying to push the thoughts away. She had to focus on studying for now.

* * *

DeeAnn and Sheila walked into a small, brightly lit room with a sign reading "Support Group for Caregivers" hanging above the door. The room had chairs arranged in a circle, with a table in the center holding a stack of pamphlets and informational brochures. The caregivers had already taken their seats, all looking tired and stressed.

"This is it," DeeAnn said as they entered the room. She hoped this group would be helpful to them.

DeeAnn looked at Sheila, who was nervously rubbing her hands together.

"Are you okay?" DeeAnn asked.

Sheila shook her head. "I don't know if I'm ready for this," she said. "What if they think I'm horrible because I am struggling?"

DeeAnn put her arm around Sheila's shoulders. "They will understand what you're going through, and no one will judge you."

As they took their seats, the group leader, a kind-looking woman named Miranda, introduced herself and explained what they would do today. "We're here to listen, share experiences, and offer advice and support to one another. I'm glad you could all make it. Let's start by going around the room and introducing ourselves."

Each caregiver took turns speaking. They talked about the challenges of caring for loved ones with Alzheimer's, the frustrations of dealing with memory loss and confusion, and the sadness of watching someone they loved slowly slip away.

Deeann and Sheila listened, nodding in understanding.

They shared their experiences, the good days and the bad, the moments that brought them joy and the moments that broke their heart.

As the meeting drew to a close, Miranda handed out brochures and thanked everyone for coming.

"What did you think?" DeeAnn asked Sheila as they got in the car.

"It was really helpful," Sheila said.

DeeAnn smiled. "I'm glad we came," she said. "We'll come back next week. In the meantime, please let me know if there's anything I can help you with."

Sheila squeezed DeeAnn's hand and smiled. "I don't think I could do this without you. You came into our life at just the right time," she said.

"I know it will not be easy," DeeAnn said, taking a deep breath. "But I'm grateful that we can do this together. We can be strong for each other and the people we love."

DeeAnn wiped away a tear as she thought about all the things she wished she could do for their father. She wished she could make him better, take away his confusion and frustration. But she knew that was impossible. All she could do was be there for him, love him, and make sure he was safe and cared for.

As she sat there, lost in thought, she felt a gentle hand on her shoulder. It was Sheila, looking tired and worried but also determined.

"We're doing the best we can," Sheila said softly. "We can't do everything, but we're doing what we can to make sure he is okay."

DeeAnn smiled at her sister. She knew she was right. They were doing everything in they could, and that was enough.

CHAPTER 8

The smell of roasted chicken filled the air as the family gathered around Mary Elle and Thomas' house. It was Sunday dinner, and everyone was excited to get together and spend some time together.

"You made it!" Mary Elle said. She was happy to see David and Tiffany join them.

She had spent all morning preparing food for their families Sunday dinner. The family kept growing, and Mary Elle couldn't help but thank God for all of them.

"Mom, what happened to your hair?" Tiffany asked, laughing.

Mary Elle rolled her eyes. "Your aunt happened!"

DeeAnn laughed from the living room. "Hey, don't blame me!"

Thomas came over and wrapped an arm around Mary Elle. "She looks as beautiful as ever."

"Your aunt lent me her hair blow dryer bonnet. She promised it would make my hair curly."

"I did not! You asked if you could borrow it, and I said yes," DeeAnn said, walking over to defend herself.

"I asked if it would make my hair curly, and you said yes."

"No, I said that if your hair is curly, then yes, it will curl."

Tiffany and Melanie giggled while they tried to fix Mary Elle's hair.

Michael joined them. "It looks good. Very 80s. All you need is a leotard and some leg warmers."

Mary Elle laughed. She loved having all her family together. "Very funny. Enough with my crazy hair. Let's have dinner."

Everyone quickly made their way to the dinner table. As they passed plates around, the conversation flowed between them. Bill filled everyone in on life now that he was retired. He told them about his latest fishing trip with Bob and some old friends. DeeAnn shared stories and pictures of Sadie and talked about how much she loved being a mother. Michael told everyone how much he loved being back in Atlanta and working on his relationship with Bill and Ruby.

Mary Elle dabbed at the corner of her eyes. "That makes me so happy, Michael."

Michael glanced at Ruby, and they smiled, making Mary Elle's heart soar. She loved seeing them together.

Michael cleared his throat. "There's something we need to tell you."

Everyone turned to look at him, and anticipation filled the room.

"We're expecting!" Ruby said.

A chorus of cheers and gasps filled the room as the family jumped up from their seats to hug them. Dinner continued for hours as everyone sat around the table, conversing. The love in the room was palpable. As Mary Elle glanced around, she couldn't help but feel so lucky. Their family had gone through so much, but they had gotten through it together. Here she was, having dinner with her ex-husband and his mistress. Her life was nothing like she had imagined it would be, but she couldn't be any happier.

*　*　*

It had been a month since the last time DeeAnn visited her father. She always tried to come more often, but getting away with a newborn wasn't easy. Gregory enjoyed spending time with his granddaughter, Sadie. Sheila said he always talked about Sadie for hours after they left. DeeAnn placed Sadie's diaper bag and stroller in the car. She then placed Sadie in her car seat and went to visit Gregory. After going to the support class for caregivers, she understood what her sister, Sheila, was going through more. Gregory's memory loss had worsened, and she was afraid he wouldn't recognize her, Sheila, or any other family member one day. It was as if she was fighting against time and would soon run out of time to make memories or cherish moments with her father. Every visit, she asked him questions about his life to get to know him better and pass along those stories to Sadie. They took a lot of photos and videos. Photos and videos of Gregory doing arts and crafts, spending time with Sadie, of him telling jokes, and drawing.

DeeAnn went to the living room, where Gregory sat on the sofa reading the newspaper. He was trying to figure out the crossword puzzle.

"Hi, Dad. How are you?" DeeAnn said as she walked into the room with Sadie in the stroller.

"DeeAnn, Sadie, welcome home," Gregory said with a warm, gentle smile.

Seeing that Gregory still recognized them and remembered their names was a relief. Today was a good day. His mind was clearer than most days, and he seemed energetic.

Sheila smiled, witnessing their interaction and how quickly he recognized DeeAnn.

"You came on a good day," Sheila confirmed with a smile.

"I'm glad to hear that. How are you holding up?"

"Dad and I were just reading the newspaper while we enjoyed some tea," Sheila said, smiling.

"Here's Sadie," DeeAnn said as she placed Sadie on her father's lap.

"You're getting big, Miss Sadie," Gregory said as he looked her over and smiled.

"She's growing up so fast, Dad. Soon she'll be walking and talking," DeeAnn said as she took her cell phone out to take photos and videos of today's visit.

"I'm glad you came to visit. I missed seeing you. Where's Paul?" Gregory asked.

"He's working today. Sorry, he couldn't make it," DeeAnn said, beaming. She couldn't believe how lucid his mind was today. She had been praying and asking God to help her father clear his mind and heal him.

"God is good," Sheila said with confidence. Sheila had also been praying to see an improvement in Gregory's mind and to have more time with her father, as his health had been declining recently.

"He truly is," DeeAnn agreed.

The visit was great. DeeAnn helped Sheila tidy up the house a bit and take care of their father. Sheila could relax and enjoy the visit as well. Sometimes, DeeAnn wanted to stay overnight to help her sister take care of their father, but with Sadie, it made it difficult. DeeAnn planned to ask Mary Elle if she could look after Sadie for a long weekend so she could spend time with her father and help Sheila, who had been struggling with the stress of taking care of their father. Sheila had devoted her time over the last year to solely caring for him. Gregory didn't like going to the doctor or having nurses enter the house. Sheila was the caregiver, and she loved it, but it also took a toll on her emotionally. She had seen Gregory go from a strong, hardworking man to a confused and lost man who needed help to find his way around the house. Recently, Gregory wandered out of the house and was missing for several hours. Sheila had called the police to help locate her father. They found Gregory in a field in the town over. It was a miracle they found him alive and well. Ever since that day, Sheila had moved into her childhood house and promised never to leave his side again. She quit her job and even lost her fiancé because of this decision, but she wouldn't have any other way.

"Thanks for visiting us," Sheila said with her voice breaking. "I don't know what we would do without you."

"I'm always here for you, and I promise I'll visit again and stay overnight," DeeAnn said as she hugged her sister and father.

* * *

Lorraine felt like she was going to pass out. Everything she had worked so hard for meant nothing now. She felt her blood boil as she pulled into her driveway and saw Christian. He was probably the last person she wanted to see right now. She angrily wiped away the tears that streamed down her face. Christian ran over to her car and motioned for her to open the passenger door, but she shook her head.

"Please, we need to talk," he said.

Lorraine shook her head. "Leave me alone."

"Lorraine, please. I know you're upset, but we need to talk. I'll wait for you on the porch. Take your time."

Lorraine sat in the car for a few more minutes. Once she felt like she was calm enough, she got out of the car.

Christian stood as soon as he saw her. "Are you okay?"

His hair was a disheveled mess, and she fought the urge to run her hands through it.

"I told you someone would see us."

"I know. It's a small town. Someone was bound to see us together. What are we supposed to do? Never go out in public? We're not doing anything wrong."

Lorraine sat on the front steps, feeling defeated. "You don't understand."

"Then help me understand," he said gently, sitting beside her.

Lorraine turned to face him. "No one's ever believed in me before... I've never believed in me before."

"I believe in you..."

"The first thing Jade said when she saw me today was that the only reason I aced my exams was because I was dating a professor."

"She doesn't know what she's talking about."

"I got every single question right in my microbiology midterm because I studied hard. I worked hard for my grade."

"I know you did. I saw you making all those index cards and study guides."

"Everyone thinks it's because of you. No one believes I could get that grade on my own. She said she was joking, but I know that they all believe her," Lorraine said as she anxiously peeled off her nail polish.

Christian took her hands in his. "Lorraine..."

"Yes?"

"Jade is your friend. You don't think there's any possibility she was joking and maybe a little jealous about your grade?"

"It doesn't matter. As long as we're together, this is how it will be."

"What are you saying?"

"I think it's best if we end things. I don't want people questioning my grades or my abilities. I don't want them to think I get special treatment because of you."

"You don't get any special treatment because of me. I'm not even one of your professors."

"I know that, but others don't know that. I want to be proud of the things that I achieve. I want to get into the nursing program because I worked hard to get in. I want people to recognize what I do."

Christian nodded sadly. "I understand that. I wish things could be different, but I respect your decision."

"Thank you," Lorraine said as her hurt broke into a million pieces.

Christian kissed her forehead. "This doesn't change how I feel about you. Whenever you're ready... you know where to find me."

CHAPTER 9

The small town was excited that the annual country fair had arrived. Patricia had been looking forward to this night all week. She was going on a third date with Anderson, Jasper's cousin. She enjoyed getting to know him and spending time with him.

"Do you want to grab something to eat first? I'm starving!" Anderson said.

As they walked through the fairgrounds, the scent of cotton candy and fried food filled the air.

Patricia smiled and nodded excitedly. "Yes! I love the curly fries here."

Patricia and Anderson approached a food vendor and ordered hot dogs, curly cheese fries, and fried Oreos. As they sat down at a picnic table to enjoy their meal, Anderson asked, "So, do you come here every year?"

Patricia took a bite of her hot dog and shook her head. "No, I haven't been here since high school. What about you?"

Anderson grinned. "I've been coming to this fair since I was a kid but haven't been in a couple of years. It's always been my favorite."

They spent the next half hour eating their food and making conversation. Patricia learned that Anderson had grown up in Winding Creek and spent the summer in Willow Heights with Jasper's family.

"This is great," said Anderson, licking ketchup off his fingers. "I'm so glad Jasper set us up."

"Yeah, me too," agreed Patricia, sipping her soda. "So, what do you want to do next?"

Anderson gestured to a nearby game booth. "Let's try our luck at that one. Maybe I can win you a prize."

They played a few games, laughing and teasing each other as they tried to toss rings around bottles and knock down targets. Eventually, Anderson won a stuffed bear, which he handed to Patricia. "Here you go, my lady," he said, bowing dramatically.

Patricia giggled as she took the bear. "Thank you, kind sir," she said, kissing his cheek.

They wandered around the fair and ended up at the petting zoo. They spent some time petting the animals and taking silly selfies with them.

Suddenly, they heard someone call out their names. They turned to see Jasper and Britney walking hand in hand.

"Hey, guys!" Patricia said, waving back. "What are you all doing here?"

"We heard there was a fair going on, so here we are," Britney said, taking a bite of her cotton candy. "What about you two?"

"Just on a date," said Anderson, putting his arm around Patricia's waist.

"Ooh, a date!" teased Britney, wiggling her eyebrows.

As Patricia and Anderson walked away, she leaned her head on his shoulder. "This has been such a fun night," she said, feeling content and happy.

At the night's end, as Patricia and Anderson walked

towards his car, they suddenly bumped into Dean, who was packing his food truck nearby. Patricia wasn't sure if she was imagining things, but she noticed his expression and immediately became sad when he saw her with someone else.

"Hey, Patty," he said, his voice tight. "I didn't know you were here."

"Hi, Dean," Patricia said, trying to keep her voice light. "This is Anderson, a friend of mine."

"We know each other," Anderson said. He extended his hand. "Nice seeing you again."

Dean shook his hand, but his eyes remained on Patricia. "You look happy," he said softly.

Patricia nodded, feeling uncomfortable. "Yeah. We had a great time at the fair."

Dean nodded but said nothing else. After an awkward silence, they said their goodbyes and went their separate ways.

On the car ride home, Patricia was quiet, lost in thought. Anderson noticed her mood and asked, "Is everything okay?"

Patricia sighed. "Yeah, I'm fine." She said, but she couldn't get Dean out of her mind.

Whenever she thought she was moving on, she saw him again, and all those feelings came rushing back.

"You deserve to be happy, Patricia. I know it hasn't been that long since ya'll broke up, but I really like you, and I'm willing to wait until you figure things out."

Patricia smiled at him, feeling grateful for his understanding. "Thanks, Anderson. I'm glad we came tonight. It was really fun."

"Me too," he said, smiling back at her. "Let's do it again soon, okay?"

"Definitely," she said, trying to push any doubt and uncertainty to the back of her mind.

* * *

"Go, Wildcats! Go, Wyatt!" Lorraine cheered on.

Wyatt's team was going against a big-shot school. Wyatt and his team were winning and making their little town proud.

It had been days since Lorraine ended her relationship with Christian. She missed him, and she knew Wyatt missed him, too. They bonded and even practiced playing basketball. Christian had promised Wyatt he would come to watch his game. Lorraine felt someone staring at her, and she turned around. She saw Christian looking at her from a distance. He had shown up on his own to watch Wyatt. Lorraine quickly looked away, but she felt butterflies in her stomach.

Lorraine had been meditating on what had happened with Christian and their relationship. She confronted herself and realized she was irrational about placing her worth and value based on her grades and career. Lorraine had never cared about other people's opinions about her, but now that she was moving into greater things in her life, it felt like she had to work extra hard to keep up with the positive image she was creating for herself. She felt her hard work and dedication at school would not be enough to prove herself as a nurse or even an outstanding student.

Had she made the right decision by ending her relationship with Christian? He was one of the good guys, and she would miss out on having someone who truly cared for her and Wyatt. It had broken Lorraine's heart when she told Wyatt that it was over between her and Christian. The look on Wyatt's face made the pain worse. Was she self-sabotaging again? Things were going extremely well, and now it was over. Why was Christian here? Could he have really meant what he said that he would be there for her if she changed her mind about them?

The Wildcats won the game. It was another victory for Willow Heights. They were the underdogs. No one ever thinks they have a chance at winning, but they always prove themselves. The scouts approached Wyatt and their coach, Mr. Peachtree. Lorraine, Mary Elle, Thomas, and Rosie walked over to the exit door by the boy's locker room to wait for Wyatt. They were all so proud of him.

"I saw Christian earlier. Did he leave already?" Mary Elle asked. She wasn't aware of the breakup, although she suspected they might have been more than friends.

"Oh, I guess he left already," Lorraine replied as she looked around.

"Wyatt told us about their fishing trip. He had an amazing time," Thomas added.

Wyatt lived with the Clarke's but would spend some weekends over at Lorraine's house. Mary Elle and Thomas had adopted Wyatt while Lorraine was figuring out her life. When she came back to Willow Heights, they worked things out and have been co-parenting Wyatt. It has been such a blessing for Lorraine to have Mary Elle and Thomas caring for her him.

"It was a great trip," Lorraine said with a sad smile.

"Is everything alright?" Mary Elle asked as she placed a hand on Lorraine's shoulder.

"Yes, everything's ok. We broke up," Lorraine shared.

"Oh, I'm sorry, honey. I did not know," Mary Elle said as she hugged Lorraine.

"Thanks, Mary Elle. I needed that hug," Lorraine said as she smiled.

"It's no problem. I'm always here in case you need anything," Mary Elle said, giving her hand a squeeze.

"Great game," Rosie said excitedly as Wyatt approached them.

"Thanks for coming, guys. It means a lot to me," Wyatt said, smiling widely.

"Nice moves, kid," Thomas said as he stole the basketball from Wyatt.

"I used your signature move," Wyatt said, running after Thomas to steal the back.

"Those two, they love to play," Mary Elle said as they walked behind them.

Rosie ran and caught up to them. She tried to steal the ball from Thomas but was too slow.

"How does Wyatt still have the energy to keep playing?" Lorraine asked with a small laugh.

"Boys will be boys," Mary Elle replied as they sat on the bleachers again.

Suddenly, Christian appeared out of nowhere and joined them at the court. He teamed up with Rosie and helped her make a three-point shot.

"I guess he hadn't left," Lorraine said with a small smile. Her heart was beating faster and harder.

"What happened between you guys, if you don't mind me asking," Mary Elle said.

"Well, he was my tutor and helped me a lot. My grades have improved tremendously, but my friend Jade asked me about my relationship with him, and I guess I felt as if she was trying to say I'm passing my classes because of him. Christian isn't my professor in any of my classes. I don't want people saying I'm passing or getting into the Nursing program because of him, so I ended our relationship. I feel like I lost my best friend and boyfriend. I think I made a mistake," Lorraine said, holding back tears as she watched the man. She loved playing basketball with her son and friends.

"Oh, honey. If he's not your professor in any classes, how

can you pass tests and classes because of him?" Mary Elle said, trying to make sense of things.

"I know, that's what I'm realizing now," Lorraine said.

"Maybe you should have clarified that with your friend. You're passing classes and exams on your own because you are putting in the time to study and working hard to achieve your goals," Mary Elle said.

"Yes, that's what I'm doing. I don't want the town to think badly of me again. I know I've messed up before and made the wrong choices, but I have worked hard this time," Lorraine added.

"I know that. We have seen the change and growth in you. You know the truth. You have nothing to prove to anyone but yourself. He's here for you, too, you know. It's not just Wyatt he cares about," Mary Elle said as she looked over at the court where they had been playing basketball.

"You're right. Now, I feel embarrassed. I don't know what to say to him. I think I messed things up between him and me for good," Lorraine said as she looked down at her hands.

"I think it'll be if it is meant to be. Just talk things out," Mary Elle said, smiling.

* * *

DEAN WAS RUSHING to set up his food truck. He had a rough night and ran late for the lunch hour rush. His employee, Vincent, is also running late. He's in a bit of a rush to set up for the day. He's pulling things out of his truck when he bumps into Thomas.

"Dean! It's good to see you."

"Thomas, hey! Sorry I didn't see you there."

Thomas peers over his shoulder. "No worries. I see you're in a bit of a rush. Do you need some help?"

"Yeah. I'm running behind, and Vincent texted me. He's running behind as well."

"Tell me what to do, and I'll help you."

He was surprised and taken aback. "Are you sure?"

"Yeah. David can hold things down at Willow Acres."

"Alright. I appreciate it," Dean said and quickly got to work with Thomas by his side.

They took care of the lunch rush easily and could soon take a break.

Thomas put an arm around Dean's shoulders. "You're really making a name for yourself, Dean. I'm proud of you."

Dean smiled. "it's going great, actually. We've been getting more and more customers every day. It's been hard work, but it's paying off."

"That's amazing to hear. I'm very happy for you."

There's a moment of silence between them before Dean sighs and looks down.

"To be honest, I feel like something's missing."

Thomas looks over at him, concerned. "What is it?"

"It's Patty. I miss her. I know I messed things up, but I can't stop thinking about her."

Thomas places a comforting hand on Dean's shoulders. "Sometimes people need a brief break before they can come back together again. It's not because there's no love, but maybe you were going in different directions at that point in time, and that's okay."

"I just can't help feeling like I screwed everything up. I didn't appreciate her the way I should have."

"Have you mentioned any of this to her?"

"No," Dean said, shaking his head.

"Then what are you doing here telling me? You're being too hard on yourself. Patty still loves you. Stop thinking about it and start acting on it. Go get your girl."

"You think so?"

Thomas nods. "Oh, yeah. So does Mary Elle, and she's always right about these sorts of things."

Dean smiled. "Thanks, Thomas. I feel better already."

"It's all in a day's work. Now, I have to get to work. Enjoy the rest of your day. Chin up!"

* * *

"Good morning," Britney said as she snuck up on Jasper, who was having a cup of coffee in a garden at Willow Acres.

Britney had finally moved to Willow Heights and visited Jasper as much as possible at work. Some would say she worked there too, but she was visiting and getting inspiration for her blog. She was also writing about small-town living and her moving process. It had a large following, as it seemed many city dwellers wanted to know how it would be to move from an urban area to a semi-rural town. Britney enjoyed telling her readers all about the fun and quaint experiences she'd have, as well as some hardships. She truly missed having big retail stores around but also realized that some things she had were unnecessary. She had been learning about repurposing things and minimizing and decluttering.

"Good morning, beautiful. I wasn't expecting you so early," Jasper said with a smile as he got up and hugged and kissed Britney.

Jasper had been over the moon to have Britney living in town. He had helped her pack and move into the house next door to Mary Elle and Thomas. It was a small house, but Britney had all the needed space. It was a bigger place than hers back in New York City and for a fraction of the rental price. Britney had been busy planting flowers and creating her own vegetable garden. She often made videos of herself working on her new garden, which she did not know she would enjoy so much. Her readers and viewers alike enjoyed seeing her go from corporate city girl to country girl, who was now learning to grow her own food in her backyard.

"I couldn't wait to see you and spend some time with you. I also have some questions about growing tomatoes," Britney said as she joined Jasper in the garden with her cup of matcha.

"What's on your mind?" Jasper asked.

"I have tried to grow them, but they keep failing to thrive."

"Have you been watering them daily? It's been pretty dry out lately. They might need more watering than usual," Jasper replied.

"I guess that's it. I was afraid to over-water them. I had been watering them every other day. I'll give that a try," Britney said with a smile. She would have to let her readers know tomatoes must be watered daily, especially if the soil was too dry.

"Got any plans today?" Jasper asked as he grabbed her hand.

"No, what do you have in mind?"

"I wanted to know if you wanted to take a nice long horse ride this afternoon. The weather's nice, and the flowers are in bloom. Riding by the lake and having a nice picnic would be nice. What do you say?" Jasper asked, hoping Britney would like his idea.

"Of course. I'll come by later on, and we can go."

"Sounds like a plan. Don't worry about packing for the picnic. I've got everything planned out."

"Great. I can't wait," Britney said and planted a big kiss on his cheek.

Later that afternoon, Britney arrived and filmed the barn area at Willow Acres when she heard hooves and turned to see Jasper. He wore jeans, a white T-shirt, boots, and his cowboy hat.

"Looking good," Britney said as she continued to live stream her vlog.

"Thanks. Oh, am I on camera?" Jasper asked, confused. He was still getting used to being in Britney's videos.

"Yes, say hello to all the viewers," Britney said, smiling.

Jasper smiled and waved. "Hello, everyone."

"Today, Jasper and I will ride horses by the lake and have a picnic. This is Twilight," Britney said as she focused the camera on the black horse Jasper was mounting a saddle on.

"Midnight is a very gentle ride. He is four years old and loves apples," Jasper said, introducing Midnight to the audience.

"This over here is Marshmallow," Britney said as she turned to the camera to film the white and gray horse next to Midnight. This is Jasper's favorite horse. She's adorable and has the sweetest personality.

Soon, the couple was on their way to the lake. Britney took the time to film all the beautiful flowers blooming and the butterflies flyings around, and she captured one landing on her hand. Viewers were commenting on how beautiful and peaceful Willow Heights was and how dreamy and surreal it seemed.

When they reached the top of the hill by the lake, they found the perfect place to picnic. Britney laid out the blanket, and Jasper put out the basket with their lunches and drinks. Britney had set her camera to film while they enjoyed their lunch and the tranquil view of the lake. It was a virtual date; everyone was there but from a distance. Britney then took close-up videos of the trees, the fields, the flowers, the lake, and even the beautiful clouds in the sky.

The viewers left a lot of positive comments and gave her Livestream video likes. This gave both Britney and Jasper lots of joy. After the live stream ended, Jasper turned to Britney and said, "I can't believe we live-streamed our date. It was strange, but I guess people enjoy sharing moments like that with you."

"Yes, there are lots of positive comments and questions about the location, the horses, and of you," Britney said with a smile.

"I guess I'm famous now," Jasper said with a small laugh as he blushed.

"You've always been famous in my book," Britney said as she hugged him.

CHAPTER 10

Mary Elle, and Rita sat on a park bench on the town square, watching Ryder and Liam playing nearby in the playground. They chatted and caught up on each other's lives.

"How's everything going with Emma?" Mary Elle asked, concerned.

Rita sighed. "It's been tough. Bob was upset when he learned about that guy sneaking into our house. But he understands Emma wasn't in an easy situation. She's been struggling more than we knew, adjusting to being back, and we're doing our best to support her."

Mary Elle nodded. "I'm glad to hear that you're there for her. She's lucky to have a family like you."

"We'll do whatever it takes to help her get through this."

"Speaking of family, how are Emma's kids doing?"

"They are doing so well. Alexander is thriving in his career and being a father. Mandy is doing very well in school. Andrew is a workaholic, but he's doing well. Having Emma back has made a tremendous impact on their life. They needed her."

Mary Elle smiled. "That's so good to hear. You have a lot to be grateful for."

They watched as Ryder and Liam ran around the playground playing tag.

Mary Elle laughed. "Can you believe it? We're grandmothers now!"

Rita chuckled. "I know. I never thought I'd see the day. Yet, here we are, sitting on a park bench, watching our grandkids run around."

Mary Elle shook her head in disbelief. "It's crazy how time flies. It feels like just yesterday we were running around on the playground."

They watched Ryder and Liam run over to them, out of breath and grinning from ear to ear. "Grandma, grandma! Did you see me? I climbed the monkey bars!" Ryder exclaimed.

Mary Elle clapped and cheered for him. "You were amazing! We're so proud of you!" Mary Elle said, giving Ryder a high five.

Rita turned to Mary Elle. "You know, being a grandmother isn't so bad. We get to spoil them, do all the fun stuff, and then send them home to their parents."

Mary Elle laughed. "That's true. No dealing with sleepless nights or dirty diapers."

As Mary Elle and Rita continued to talk and watch the boys, Mrs. Adelman joined them.

"What brings you here today, Mrs. Adelman?" Mary Elle asked.

"Oh, you know, just getting my steps in," she responded.

"It's a lovely day to be outside," Rita said.

"Have you heard the hot gossip going around?" Mrs. Adelman asked with a sly smile.

Mary Elle and Rita leaned in, intrigued. "No, what is it?" Mary Elle asked.

Mrs. Adelman lowered her voice. "Well, rumor has it that our lovely town veterinarian has a new love interest."

Mary Elle smiled. "That's great! She is such a lovely girl."

Rita nodded in agreement. "She's a sweetheart. Penny loves her."

They continued to chat and catch up on the latest news and gossip in town. Even though Mrs. Adelman was known for being nosy, Mary Elle and Rita knew she had a good heart and cared for their community.

* * *

Patricia was excited and nervous as she set up her first booth at the farmer's market. Since she could remember, she had dreamt of owning her own flower shop, and this was the perfect opportunity to showcase her talents and make a name for herself. She had spent a long time selecting the most beautiful blooms in her garden.

As she set up her colorful blooms and created stunning floral arrangements, she couldn't help but feel a sense of pride. This was her time to shine, and she couldn't wait to see what the day would bring. She had put a lot of thought and love into her arrangements and hoped they would attract plenty of customers.

Just as she finished setting up the last of her flowers, she glanced up to see Dean walking toward her. She had known there was a possibility that they would bump into each other, but she hadn't wanted that to hold her back. She had held herself back for far too long.

"Hey, Patty," he said, flashing a smile. "I heard you were going to be here today. I wanted to come and show my support."

Patricia felt a mix of emotions as she looked at Dean. She appreciated the gesture, but their breakup still hurt a part of her, but she wasn't one to hold grudges. "Thanks, Dean. I appreciate it."

"These are beautiful, Patty. You're very talented."

Patricia beamed with pride. "Thanks, Dean. I worked really hard on these."

Patricia couldn't help but feel a spark between them as they chatted. She had always loved Dean's easygoing personality and charming smile. Dean purchased two small floral arrangements for the picnic tables near his food truck.

After Dean left, Melanie arrived with the twins in tow. Patricia smiled as she saw her approaching. Melanie had been struggling with the three kids and finding time for herself. It was nice seeing her out and about.

"Hey, Patty! Your booth looks amazing!" Melanie exclaimed, admiring the colorful display.

"Thanks, Melanie! I'm so glad you came."

Melanie picked out a few of Patricia's favorite flowers and chatted about how things were going. Patricia filled her in on Dean passing by and how it had made her feel.

"It was strange seeing him here, but also nice. He really inspired me to follow my dream, you know? Before I dated Dean, I was kind of boy crazy and had no personal goals."

Melanie nods and laughs. "Oh, yeah, I remember. Sometimes it takes someone from our past to remind us how far we've come and how we've grown. And look how great you're doing now!"

As the day passed, Patricia's booth became a popular spot at the farmer's market. People stopped by to admire her work and placed orders for customized arrangements.

It thrilled Patricia to see the response she was getting. It was a lot of hard work, but seeing people's faces light up when they saw her creations was worth it.

Just as she was packing to leave, she saw Dean walking

towards her again. Her heart skipped a beat as she watched him approach.

"Hey, Patty," he said, flashing his handsome smile. "I just wanted to come by and see how you did today. Looks like you did pretty well!"

Patricia smiled back. "Yeah, it was a great day. I'm really happy with how everything turned out."

"Let me help you take these things to your truck," Dean said.

Patricia watched as he effortlessly grabbed things and took them to her truck. She followed close behind with a box filled with vases. She carefully put it in her car.

As they said goodbye, Dean leaned in and kissed her cheek. "I'm proud of you, Patty," he said. "You're doing great."

"Seeing you follow your dream of opening the food truck really inspired me," Patricia said.

Dean nodded, his eyes filled with pride. "I'm glad to hear that. You deserve to be happy and successful."

Patricia watched as he walked away, feeling a mixture of emotions. She didn't know what the future held for them, but she knew one thing was certain: today was a success, and this was the motivation she needed to keep chasing her dreams.

* * *

Lorraine sat on the bleachers while waiting for Wyatt to finish his basketball game with friends. They were going to have dinner with Rosie and her parents. It was very important for Wyatt that Lorraine got to know Rosie's parents and wanted to make a good impression. Lorraine was still battling her emotions and thoughts of feeling less than others. She was working on feeling proud of herself and the life she was forging for herself and Wyatt, but she still felt like everyone was constantly judging her.

Deep down, she knew it was all in her head. As time passed, she learned that good people were out there. There were people in their life that cared for them and wanted to see them succeed. It was hard to see that at first because she'd never had that. Her family had always tried to beat her when she was already down and told her that everyone was judging her. Lorraine would never understand why her family had been that way, but therapy was helping her.

Lorraine glanced at the court and almost jumped in to stop the game. Wyatt was playing with his school friends, but the opposing team had boys from Winding Creek. They were playing aggressively and spewing nonsense. Both teams were fiercely competitive, but one boy looked like he had it out for Wyatt. Even though it was not an actual game, and the boys were only shooting hoops for fun, the bleachers were full of onlookers.

The game continues, with both teams playing rough. Wyatt makes a move, trying to get past Jake. But Jake expects his move and blocks it, Wyatt's knee crashes into Jake's leg, and suddenly Wyatt falls to the ground, clutching his leg. The game comes to a complete halt. The other boys gather around him, asking if he's okay. Lorraine sprints to the court and goes straight to Wyatt. It's clear that he's badly injured as he cries out in pain.

"What happened?" she asks.

The boy Lorraine had been keeping an eye on speaks up. "I'm so sorry. I didn't mean to hurt him."

Before Lorraine can say anything else, the boy runs off with a few friends running after him.

"What happened?" Lorraine asks Wyatt's friend, Luke.

"I'm not sure. I saw Jake playing rough with Wyatt, and I think he hurt him on purpose."

"Honey, can you get up?"

"No," Wyatt says.

Lorraine notices the tears rolling down his cheeks. She grabs her cell phone and calls an ambulance.

"Everything's going to be okay," she says, hanging up the call and waiting for the ambulance to arrive.

Even though it only took them a few minutes to get to them, it felt like an eternity for Lorraine. Unable to stay still, Lorraine paces back and forth in the hospital corridor.

"Lorraine?" Mary Elle says, rushing to her side. Lorraine breaks down at the sight of Mary Elle and Thomas, and she collapses into Mary Elle's arms.

"It's okay. I know it's scary, but he's going to be okay," Mary Elle says, rubbing her back as she holds her.

When the Doctor approaches them, Lorraine feels a shiver down her back.

"What's going on, Doctor?" Thomas asks.

The Doctor pushes his glasses up his nose. "I'm afraid I have some bad news."

The room spins. Lorraine can faintly hear Thomas ask the doctor if Wyatt will be okay.

"I'm afraid he tore his ACL. We will need an MRI to confirm. We will need to perform surgery if his ACL is torn."

"This can't be happening..." Mary Elle says.

"Is his basketball career over?" Lorraine asks.

"It's too soon to say, but it is a possibility. An injury like this can end careers. It depends on how well he does with the treatment."

"We still don't know if it's his ACL. Can we not mention it to him yet?" Thomas asks.

"Sure."

Mary Elle hugs Lorraine, offering her comfort and support. Lorraine is thankful to have them here with her. She knows that they have Wyatt's best interest at heart as well.

CHAPTER 11

It was a beautiful spring day when Patricia bumped into Dean on her way to work. She was in a better mood than usual after her date. She hadn't seen Dean since the last time she bumped into him, and she couldn't help the sadness that hit her when she saw him. Even after all this time, she still missed him.

"Hey, Patty," Dean exclaimed, smiling.

"Hi, Dean," Patricia replied, feeling a little awkward. "How are you?"

"I'm good, thanks. How about you?" Dean asked, his eyes lingering on her face, making her blush.

"I'm doing alright," she said, sounding casual.

"That's good," Dean replied. "I've been keeping busy with work and stuff."

Patricia nodded, not sure what to say. There was a brief silence before Dean spoke up again.

"Patty," he said. "I know things ended badly between us, but I've been thinking about it lately, and I think we should talk."

Her heart skipped a beat. She had been hoping for this

moment for a long time but didn't want to appear too eager. Besides, she had gone on a date, and it had gone well. Maybe Dean was just too little too late.

"Sure," she said, trying to keep her voice steady. "I think that would be a good idea."

"Great," Dean said, smiling. "How about we meet up for coffee tomorrow evening? "

Patricia smiled back, feeling a little more at ease. "Sounds good," she said. "What time?"

"How about six o'clock?"

"Okay, six it is," Patricia said, trying to hide her excitement. "I'll see you there."

Patricia stood stuck in place as she watched Dean walk away. She couldn't help but feel a sense of anticipation. Maybe this was the opportunity they needed to patch things up and move forward. Or maybe it was just a chance to say goodbye once and for all. Dean turned around and smiled when their eyes met. Patricia quickly turned around and went on her way.

The next day, Patricia arrived at the café a few minutes early and ordered a latte and a blueberry donut. She sat at a small table by the window and waited nervously for Dean to arrive. As she sipped her coffee, she couldn't help but feel a little anxious. What if things didn't go well? What if they ended up arguing again?

Just as she was about to let her nerves get the best of her, Dean walked through the door. He looked even more handsome than she remembered. Dean spotted Patricia, and his eyes lit up. He walked over to her table, a smile on his face.

"Hey," he said, sitting down across from her. "Thanks for coming."

"No problem," Patricia replied, trying to sound casual but unable to control how her heart was almost beating out of her chest. Maybe she shouldn't have come so early. She didn't want him to think she was desperate.

They sat there making small talk about work and the weather. Despite everything between them, Patricia couldn't help but notice how comfortable she felt around Dean. She liked the way she felt around him. He told her about the food truck and how well everything was going.

"Yeah, I've tried a few things from your food truck, and they were very good."

"You have?" he asked in disbelief.

"Of course. I might not go myself, but I've had people pick things up for me when they've gone. It was my small way of showing support from afar."

"Thanks. That means a lot to me."

"So, Dean," she said, taking a deep breath. "What did you want to talk about?"

Dean looked at her, his expression serious. "Patty, I know we've had our differences in the past, but I want you to know that I'm sorry for how things ended between us. I've been thinking a lot about what went wrong, and I think we can work through it if we try."

She looked at him with a mixture of surprise and hope in her eyes. Patricia felt her heart racing. This was it–the moment she had been waiting for.

"I want that too, Dean," she said, her voice shaking slightly. " I've been seeing someone else, but I know it's not what I want. I've missed you."

Dean's face lights up, and he reaches across the table to take her hand. Patricia smiles, feeling relief wash over her. Maybe this was the beginning of something new — something better than before.

As they talked and laughed over coffee, Patricia felt a sense of hope for the first time in a long time. Maybe, just maybe, they could make things work this time around. They chatted for the next few hours, catching up on each other's lives and remembering old times. Patricia laughed at Dean's jokes and realized how much she had missed him. Dean hadn't only been a boyfriend; he had been a friend and coworker, and when things ended between them, it had been so hard for that very reason.

* * *

MELANIE ARRIVED at the location for her first engagement shot since she returned to work from maternity leave. The shoot was at Willow Acres, and the weather was perfect for a spring shoot in the mountains. As she set up her equipment, she couldn't help but feel excited. Melanie loved capturing beautiful moments for couples that they could cherish forever.

The clients arrived, and Melanie greeted them with a warm smile. She explained the plan for the shoot and asked them to post in different positions. The shots were turning out great, and the clients were cooperative.

After wrapping up the shoot, Melanie sat down with Lisa and Bailey to catch up on everything she missed during her leave.

"Not going to lie, it was pretty boring without you here," Bailey said.

"That's true," Lisa said. "Have you heard about Gemma?"

"No, what about her?"

Bailey leaned over and said in a hushed tone, "Supposedly, she's been looking for other jobs."

"She is? Why?" Melanie asked.

"She had a crush on Jasper," Lisa said. "It's difficult having to work with someone you had feelings for and see their girlfriend around all the time."

Bailey laughed. "Speak of the devil."

Britney walked towards them, looking cute in her jean overalls and high ponytail. She seemed to fit in just fine.

"Hey, Britney! What brings you by?" Melanie asks.

"I'm just here to see Jasper. I thought I'd also stop by and say hi to you guys."

As they continued to chat, Britney mentioned she had been keeping up with her social media accounts and garnered even more followers.

"You guys won't believe it, but my followers love the new content. They're really into the small-town life and the whole 'city girl meets country boy' thing."

"That's great news! What kind of feedback are you getting?" Lisa asks.

"They love Jasper. They call him a sexy cowboy and always ask for more pictures and videos of him."

Melanie laughs. "That's hilarious! I can't believe you're turning Jasper into an influencer."

"I know! Jasper has always been so private, but I think he's getting into it now."

"I love having you here and seeing you settling in so well," Melanie says.

Britney nods. "It's been a big change, but it's been rewarding, and I love this life."

"You're like a natural country girl now," Bailey says.

Britney smiles. "Who knows, maybe one day we'll have a little cowboy or cowgirl of our own."

Everyone laughs at Britney's comment, but Melanie can't stop smiling, seeing how happy and secure she seems now. Before moving to Willow Heights, it always seemed like Britney was putting on an act. These days she was genuinely happy. It truly seemed like Britney had found her place in the world. Melanie was so happy to see her friend so content and at ease, making her reflect on her life. Melanie had been so stressed about managing work and her family that she was starting not to enjoy anything anymore. After seeing Britney so happy and finding joy in the simple things, she made a mental note to take a step back and appreciate her life more. She had to remember that happiness could be found in unexpected places.

* * *

It had been months since Tiffany and David returned from their honeymoon. Things were going great. They were still adjusting to living together. Tiffany and David enjoyed cooking and folding the laundry together.

"I love how warm the clothing comes out of the dryer," Tiffany said as she folded a shirt.

"It's toasty," David said, smiling.

"I can't believe it's been a month of us being married and living together. It's been the best month of my life," Tiffany said with a big smile on her face.

"It's been wonderful. The years to come will be even better," David said as he leaned into Tiffany and kissed her on her lips.

Tiffany felt loved. Although things weren't perfect, she knew there wasn't a problem she and David couldn't conquer together. They were learning about each other's little quirks and habits and becoming more comfortable with each other more and more than the days went by. They were patient with each other's flaws.

They had a morning routine established. They loved having breakfast together and often sat on their back porch with their first cup of coffee and shared their plans for the day. In the evenings, they loved to cook together, and after dinner, they enjoyed working out in their home gym, which was finally finished. On the weekends, they loved to sleep in and visit friends and family together. Life was grand. They had each other.

"I invited Jasper and Britney over for dinner tomorrow," Tiffany said.

"I didn't know Britney was back in town," David replied as he continued to fold towels.

"She's flying in today. Jasper is super excited," Tiffany said as she got up to put their clothing in the drawers.

"Are we going out or hosting them?" David asked.

He had been waiting for weeks for the opportunity to fire up the new grill he had just purchased.

"We could host it here and use your new grill," Tiffany said with a smile. She knew he was excited to use it for the first time.

"Sounds like a great idea to me. I'll go buy some meat and veggies to grill," David said with excitement overflowing. He was like a kid with a brand-new toy.

"I'll let Britney know," Tiffany said as she grabbed her phone and texted Britney.

"Maybe we should invite Melanie and Cade over too? And Sienna and Kyle?"

Tiffany kissed David on the lips. "Our first time hosting all our friends."

CHAPTER 12

Patricia walks into the Busy Bee Coffee shop and looks around for Anderson. She smiles and walks over when she spots him sitting at a table in the corner.

"Hey Anderson, how's it going?" she asks, sitting across from him.

"Hey, good to see you. I'm good, Patty. How about you?" Anderson replies, smiling back at her.

"I'm doing pretty well. Thanks for meeting me here today."

Anderson looked up and smiled warmly at her. "Of course, it's always nice to see you," he said.

They chatted for a few minutes about the weather and local happenings, but Patricia could tell that Anderson was eager to get to the reason for their meeting.

"I actually wanted to talk to you about something, if that's okay," Patricia says, looking slightly nervous.

"Sure, what's up?" Anderson asks, his expression becoming more serious.

"Well, I just wanted to say that I've really enjoyed getting to know you over the past few weeks. You're a great guy, and I've had a lot of fun getting to know you," Patricia says, looking down at her hands.

"Thanks, Patricia. I've enjoyed spending time with you, too," he says, looking a little confused.

"But I have to be honest with you. Dean and I have been talking and decided to give our relationship a second chance. After some time apart, we feel we're in a better place now," Patricia says, her smile faltering. She hates hurting Anderson, but she knows it's for the best.

"Oh," Anderson says, his face falling slightly but quickly composing himself. "Well, I'm happy for you, Patty. I hope everything works out with Dean."

They chatted a bit more, but the conversation felt strained.

"Thanks again for meeting with me. I hope we can still be friends," Patricia says, hoping to ease the situation's awkwardness.

"Of course," Anderson says, smiling again. "I understand that sometimes things don't work out how we want them to. I'm still glad we got to know each other, and I wish you all the best."

"Thanks, Anderson. You're a really great guy," Patricia says, standing up from the table. "I'll see you around, okay?"

"Take care," Anderson says.

With that, Patricia turns and walks out of the coffee shop, feeling mixed emotions. She had just ended a new relationship and was feeling sad about it. However, she was also happy about her future with Dean. She felt grateful that they were getting a second chance at love together. Walking down the street, she noticed the beautiful blooming tulips and the fresh spring breeze. She took a deep breath and smiled, hopeful about her future with Dean.

* * *

TIFFANY STARTED her day and felt a little off. She wasn't sure what it could be. A small voice told her to check her period tracking app. It had been a few days since she was supposed to get her period. She hadn't worried about it or paid any attention to her period being late because her menstrual cycle was irregular. She had been brushing pregnancy thoughts off, but things felt a little strange now. Tiffany didn't want to hype herself up to find out she was wrong.

Throughout the day, Tiffany couldn't shake the pregnancy thoughts off. She went to the pharmacy while David was out getting groceries for the barbecue at her house. Tiffany got several tests to make sure some were digital and some were the ones that show the lines only. She went back home and waited until after dinner to take her time and take the tests in privacy and with David at home.

Soon after, David arrived home with groceries and set up the grill in the backyard. Tiffany helped him and watched him with admiration. She knew how much he enjoyed cooking and how excited he had been about using his new grill.

The doorbell rang, and it was Jasper and Britney.

"Welcome," Tiffany said as she opened the door for her friends.

"Wow, you are glowing. Married life has been good for you," Britney said as she threw her arms around her old friend Tiffany.

"Aw, thanks. Come on in. David's out in the backyard starting up the grill," Tiffany said as she guided Britney and Jasper.

Jasper jumped into action and helped David at the grill while Tiffany and Britney caught up while drinking seltzers.

The sun was shining brightly, and the smell of the barbecue was in the air.

"Are we late for the party?" Melanie asked as she and Cade joined them in the backyard by the side gate.

"Wait! What's going on?" Tiffany asked, surprised to see Patricia and Dean as well.

"We ran into these two crazy kids when we picked up dessert," Cade said.

Tiffany hugged Patricia. "You guys are back together?"

"We are."

Tiffany squealed in excitement.

David patted Dean's back. "Gangs back together."

"Sienna and Kyle will be here in a few minutes," Tiffany said as the ladies all took seats.

"So, tell us. Is married life all you imagined it would be?" Patricia asked as she sat next to Tiffany.

"It's been amazing so far! We are still adjusting to living together, but marrying David was the best thing I ever did."

Britney served some chips and queso dip on her plate. "Aw. That's so sweet. Have you gotten into any fights yet?"

"Yeah, nothing major. Just silly things like leaving the kitchen cabinets open or dirty laundry next to the laundry hamper instead of putting it inside."

Melanie laughed. "Seriously! Why is that so hard to do?"

Patricia rolled her eyes. "Men."

"They're impossible, but we can't live without them," Britney said as she dreamily gazed at Jasper.

Melanie glanced at Tiffany wide-eyed. "What is this?"

Tiffany knew exactly what it was as soon as she saw the bag she was holding. She must have brought it out with the rest of the snacks.

"Oh, my gosh. Are you pregnant?" Sienna asked as she stood frozen in place.

She and Kyle had just arrived. Kyle signaled that his lips were sealed and went over to the guys.

"I don't know yet. I haven't taken the tests, but my period is late."

All the girls surrounded Tiffany and squealed softly, keeping it a secret from David and the guys.

"When are you going to take the tests?" Melanie asked with wide eyes and a smile.

"I was going to do it after the party. I don't want to get my hopes up, and then it turns out to be nothing," Tiffany said, looking over at David, who was busy grilling chicken and talking to the guys.

"Wow, I'm so excited for you either way," Britney said, smiling.

"Thanks, ladies, but nothing is for sure yet," Tiffany said.

"I love how you and David have decorated the house," Sienna said as she sat around the fire pit. Spring nights on the mountain were chilly, and the sun was setting.

"Thanks, it's a combination of our styles," Tiffany replied as she grabbed the fruit salad bowl and placed it across them with small plates and utensils.

"How were the Maldives?" Britney asked excitedly.

"It was amazing. The resort was beautiful. The website photos don't do it justice. Thanks for recommending it and helping us get such a great discount," Tiffany said, smiling. She was clearly reliving those wonderful moments as a newlywed in her mind.

"No problem. I'm so happy you enjoyed it. The magazine has a nice contract with them for ads, and they get a lot of business through us. I'm so glad you had an amazing time. I'm trying to visit there soon; I want to surprise Jasper with a trip like that," Britney shared in a hushed tone.

"He will love it. Even David, who isn't a beachgoer, truly loved it," Tiffany replied.

* * *

"Wyatt, how are you feeling?" Lorraine asked Wyatt after they brought him back from getting a CT scan.

"I'm in pain. I guess I'm more worried about not being able to play basketball or not having a chance of being a pro player," Wyatt said as tears filled his eyes.

"I know it's a hard time for you right now, but don't forget it's in God's hands. There isn't anything impossible for him. He knows how much basketball means to you and all your hopes and dreams. I know he is in control, and we need to trust him," Lorraine said as she leaned down to kiss Wyatt on his forehead. It pained her to see him this sad and possibly lose the opportunity of receiving the basketball scholarship he was working so hard to earn. Wyatt also loved the sport, and it helped him become confident in himself and make good friends.

"Mom, did you call Chris?" Wyatt asked.

"No, I haven't spoken with him."

"Oh, because I saw him downstairs earlier when I was waiting to be seen by the doctor, and you had gone to get coffee. I thought he was looking for you because he didn't see me," Wyatt explained.

The news that Christian had shown up in the hospital shocked Lorraine. She wasn't expecting to hear that Christian had been in the hospital. She figured Mary Elle or Thomas had told him about Wyatt's injury.

"No, I didn't know he knew you had gotten injured and were in the hospital," Lorraine replied.

Lorraine was debating in her mind whether to reach out to Christian or just let it be.

"Rosie texted me. She is visiting me today," Wyatt asked, looking for his phone.

"Ok, I can't believe we have been here for two days. I'm

grateful the hospital staff has been monitoring you and doing their best," Lorraine replied.

"Dr. Reynolds said they are releasing me tomorrow once the specialist reviews my scans and they decide about the surgery," Wyatt said as he shifted on the bed.

"I know, sweetheart. I hate seeing you in pain. I wish you were out there being your usual self," Lorraine replied.

"Mom, I don't want to add more stress to you, but I think you have an upcoming test you need to study for," Wyatt said as he was checking his text messages and realized he had made a calendar event to remind him to help Lorraine study for her final exam.

"Yes, you are right. I had completely forgotten. I'll email my professor and see if she can give me a chance to take it at her office next week before the semester ends," Lorraine said as she quickly grabbed her phone and composed her email.

Things were getting hectic for Lorraine. She had so much on her mind that it felt almost impossible to concentrate enough to write an articulate email explaining to Professor Whitlock her current situation. She hoped and prayed that Professor Whitlock would understand her and give her a chance to take the test next week, giving her time to study.

CHAPTER 13

The next morning, Tiffany got up early and tiptoed into the kitchen. She carefully prepared breakfast for David. She made his favorite sunny-side-up eggs, bacon, buttermilk pancakes, and hash browns. In case he didn't want orange juice, Tiffany made freshly squeezed orange juice and coffee. She arranged everything on a tray with a small box wrapped in a white ribbon.

Tiffany went to the bedroom with the tray in hand, where David was sound asleep. She gently set the tray on his nightstand and kissed him on the lips to wake him up.

"Good morning, handsome," Tiffany said as she brushed his hair back from his forehead.

David opened his eyes and smiled at Tiffany as she held the tray. He sat up and said, "What's all this?"

"It's breakfast in bed, silly. I have a surprise for you," Tiffany said as she sat the tray over David's legs on the bed.

David grinned, looked over the tray, and found the small box with the white ribbon. "What's this?" he asked.

"That's the surprise. Open it," Tiffany said with a smile.

She was so nervous, and she hoped he would be happy once he learned about the surprise.

David carefully untied the ribbon and opened the box. Inside the box was a tiny pair of baby booties. He looked up at Tiffany in shock, not quite understanding. His heart was racing. "Are we going to be parents?" he asked.

Tiffany's eyes swelled with tears of joy, and all she could do was nod.

David couldn't believe it. He put the tray aside and got up to hug his wife. She could finally say, "Yes, I'm pregnant." It was the first time she had said it out loud, and it felt surreal. She was going to be a mother. Her love for this baby was already immense, and she couldn't wait to meet the growing baby inside her. David placed his hand over her lower abdominal area and leaned down, and said, "Hi baby, I love you. We can't wait to meet you."

David and Tiffany held each other.

He whispered to Tiffany, "I love you so much."

"I love you too. I can't wait for this new chapter in our lives together," Tiffany said as they hugged and enjoyed this special moment.

CHAPTER 14

Lorraine shivered in the dark, her breath visible in the cool air. She pulled her blanket tighter around her and hugged herself for warmth. The night was silent except for the rustling of leaves and the occasional hoot of an owl. She couldn't help but feel a sense of loneliness and despair creeping up on her. Her mind raced with worries about Wyatt's future and the uncertainty ahead.

As she sat there, lost in thought, she suddenly heard a faint rustling noise coming from the direction of her neighbor's house. She strained her eyes to see through the darkness but couldn't make anything out. Her heart raced as she wondered who or what might make the noise.

Suddenly, a figure emerged from the darkness. It was her neighbor, Rita, Mary Elle's best friend. Lorraine breathed a sigh of relief and smiled as Rita made her way over to the fence that separated their yards.

"Good evening, Lorraine," Rita said with a warm smile.

Lorraine returned the smile, grateful for the company. "Hi, Rita. It's a beautiful night, isn't it?"

"It certainly is," Rita replied. "I couldn't help but notice you sitting out here alone. Is everything okay?"

Lorraine hesitated for a moment before confiding in her. She told Rita about Wyatt's injury and the uncertainty surrounding his future in basketball. Rita listened attentively, nodding in understanding.

"I'm so sorry to hear that, Lorraine," she said softly. "But Wyatt will find his way, no matter what the future holds. And you, my dear, are stronger than you give yourself credit for."

Lorraine felt a lump in her throat as Rita's words sank in. She had always been so focused on caring for Wyatt that she hadn't taken the time to recognize her strength. Her eyes welled up with tears as she realized she needed someone to lean on.

Rita must have sensed her emotions because she placed a comforting hand on Lorraine's shoulder. "We're here for you, Lorraine. You're not alone in this."

Lorraine felt a sense of warmth and gratitude wash over her as she leaned into Rita's embrace. She didn't feel so helpless and alone for the first time in days.

As they sat together in silence, Lorraine watched as the rabbit she had seen earlier hopped by. She couldn't help but feel a sense of awe at the animal's graceful movements. It reminded her of a preaching she'd heard as a child. The Pastor said that just like birds didn't have to worry about their next meal, neither should we worry about anything because God will always provide for us. How the rabbit navigated the forest so carelessly with no worry was as if the rabbit knew that everything it needed was available, just as the Pastor had said.

Lorraine felt a renewed sense of hope wash over her. She knew that no matter what challenges lay ahead, she would overcome them.

* * *

THE SMELL of pot roast filled the air as everyone sat around the Clarke household for Sunday dinner. The family gathered around the dining table, adorned with a white tablecloth and a beautiful flower arrangement Mary Elle had purchased from Patricia.

Every plate had a helping of mashed potatoes, gravy, roasted carrots, and green beans. The sound of cutlery tapping against the dinner plates echoed throughout the room as everyone ate. The family laughed and joked as they enjoyed each other's company. When they finished their meals, they sat back, pleasantly satisfied. No one wanted to leave the table, as they were having too much fun together.

Tiffany felt extra grateful to be surrounded by everyone today. She couldn't wait to tell them she and David were expecting. She was most excited to see Ruby and Michael. They only saw them on Sunday dinners since they both lived in Atlanta. Ruby and Michael were now engaged.

Tiffany cleared her throat and glanced at David. He was smiling at her and put his arm around her shoulders.

"David and I have an announcement to make."

Everyone turned their gaze at them.

"We're so happy you're all here. We have some news to share with you."

"We're expecting!" David said.

Everyone congratulated the happy couple.

"And the best part is, we're due around the same time!" Tiffany said, glancing at Ruby.

Ruby brought a hand to her face. "No way! Remember how we used to dream about this as kids?" She turned to Melanie and squeezed her hand.

Melanie looked up from her plate, a warm smile

spreading across her face. "It's such a blessing to be a mother," she said, looking over at her three children playing in the living room.

Tiffany and Ruby shared a knowing smile. They had been best friends since they were kids, and now they were experiencing one of life's most precious moments together. Tiffany couldn't believe it. She was over the moon that she and Ruby would go through this exciting journey together. She turned to Melanie, who was now listening intently to their conversation.

"I can't wait to experience motherhood with you guys," Melanie said. "It truly is such a blessing."

Melanie had always been the nurturing type and loved being a mother. Tiffany admired her sister's patience and dedication to her family.

Mary Elle beamed with pride at her family, feeling grateful to have everyone together for Sunday dinner. "I'm so happy to have everyone together. This Sunday dinner is extra special with the news of two new babies on the way."

Tiffany smiled at her mother. "We're so lucky to have you, Mom. Thank you for always being there for us."

Ruby nods in agreement. "Yes, I truly couldn't ask for a better mother-in-law. You're always so supportive and loving."

As they enjoyed their meal, Tiffany and Ruby talked excitedly about their pregnancies, sharing tips and stories with each other. Melanie chimed in with her own experiences, offering advice and encouragement.

"I can't believe we're both pregnant, Ruby! This is going to be so much fun."

"I know. I'm so excited. And it's even better that we get to experience this together."

Throughout the meal, Tiffany couldn't help but feel

grateful for the bond she shared with Ruby. They had been best friends since they were kids, and now they were about to embark on this new adventure together. Tiffany couldn't wait for the next time they would all be together. She knew their bond would grow stronger as they went through this journey together.

CHAPTER 15

Patricia arrived at the restaurant, surprised to find the place closed to the public. She double-checked the address with the one Dean had texted her earlier. After confirming she was in the right place, she tried the door, and it opened. The place is dark, and she can't see a thing.

"Dean?" she calls out.

"Over here," comes his reply, and she follows the sound to the kitchen. She finds him standing over the stove, a pot of something delicious bubbling away. He's cooking up a storm, and the effort he's putting in blows her away.

"Dean, it smells amazing!" she exclaims, walking over to hug him.

"I wanted to do something special for you," Dean says. "You've always believed in me, even when I didn't believe in myself. None of my success would mean anything without you. Look at this place. This restaurant is mine because you believed in me."

Patricia feels tears welling up in her eyes. She has missed Dean so much, and being back in his arms feels incredible.

"I love you, Dean. I'm so proud of you," she whispers.

"I love you too, Patty," Dean replies and kisses her.

Dean takes her hand and walks her back to the restaurant as they pull apart. He turns on the lights, and Patricia's eyes widen as she takes it all in.

The restaurant was unlike anything she had ever seen before. The dim lighting that creates a sultry glow complemented the modern décor. Abstract art hung on the walls, and the tables were set with black linens and silverware.

"Dean, this place is amazing," she says.

"I know," he says. "I've been working at this place for a year now, and you're the first person to see it."

As they sat down, Dean poured them a glass of champagne. He raised his glass in a toast.

"To us," he said, looking deep into her eyes. "To our love and our future together."

She could feel his warm gaze on her as she sipped the champagne, and she knew she was exactly where she was meant to be. Dean disappears to the kitchen and returns a few moments later, carrying a food tray. He sets it down on the table and removes the lid, revealing a delicious spread of the first pasta dish he ever prepared for Patricia when they first dated.

"Dean, this is amazing," Patricia says, her eyes sparkling joyfully. "I can't believe you did all this for me."

"I would do anything for you, Patty," Dean replies, his gaze locked with her. "I know I made a mistake by letting you go, but I promise to make it up to you every day for the rest of our lives."

As they eat, they talk about everything and nothing. Their conversation flows easily and naturally. Dean tells her about his plans for the restaurant, and Patricia listens, completely engrossed in his vision.

As they leave the restaurant hand in hand, Patricia knows

that their love is stronger than ever, and she knows they're meant to be together, now and forever. This is only the beginning of their happily ever after.

* * *

Mary Elle, Tiffany, Lorraine, and Melanie arrived at Rita's house right on time. The ladies were having a night of wine and crafts. The men would spend the night playing poker and watching the kids.

"Come in, ladies!" Rita said as she swung the door open.

Sienna was right behind her with a tray of wine glasses ready and ginger ale for Tiffany. They each grabbed a glass and went to Rita's craft room.

"It's been so long since it's been just us," Melanie said as she got comfortable in her seat.

Rita nodded. "I've missed having us all together like this," she said.

The ladies gathered around the craft room, and the sound of laughter and chatter soon filled the room. The table was filled with various crafts, supplies, and empty wine glasses.

Rita and Sienna poured more wine into everyone's glasses. Rita raised her glass to toast everyone.

"Here's to good friends, wonderful wine, and good crafting!" she exclaimed.

The other ladies clinked their glasses together and took a sip.

"So, what are we making tonight?" asked Emma, Rita's sister, picking up a glittery piece of cardstock.

"I thought we could make some homemade cards," replied Tiffany. "The town council has gathered some money to give the graduating class some cash as they take off to college."

"That's so sweet," said Melanie, grabbing a stamp pad. "I have done nothing like this in ages."

"Are you ladies ready to get your crafts on?" Mary Elle asked, holding a glue gun up.

Rita took her seat. "I am! But let's try not to glue our fingers together this time?"

Mary Elle laughs. "Isn't that part of the charm of a DIY project?"

The women chatted and joked about their daily lives as they got to work. They caught up on what they had all been up to with work and life. Melanie shared stories about the kids, and Tiffany shared her honeymoon pictures. The conversation was light and easy, the kind only good friends can have.

After a while, Sienna stood up and stretched her arms. "I don't know about you guys, but I could use a snack," she said.

Rita nodded and led the way to the kitchen. She opened the fridge and pulled out a tray of cheese and crackers.

"Yum, this looks amazing," said Lorraine, taking a cracker and piling it high with cheese.

They sat around the kitchen island, munching on snacks and sipping wine. The conversation turned to more serious topics, like their goals and aspirations.

"I've been thinking that maybe I jumped the gun, ending things with Christian," said Lorraine, taking a sip of wine. "These last few days have been very hard. I'm glad we're doing this today."

The other women listened attentively, nodding and offering words of encouragement.

"Breakups are never easy. Take some time to reflect on why you ended things. Were you just scared?" Said Mary Elle.

"Yes, I think it scared me because he's such a good guy, and I didn't think I deserved him."

"You're so smart, hardworking, and beautiful. He was just as lucky to have you as you were to have him," Melanie said.

"Everything is going to work itself out," Rita said.

The rest of the evening passed in a blur of laughter, crafting, and wine. By the night's end, they had each created a handful of beautiful handmade cards and made memories that would last a lifetime.

As they hugged goodbye, Mary Elle turned to Rita and said, "Thanks for hosting this amazing ladies' night. I feel so lucky to have friends like you."

Rita smiled and hugged her back. "Anytime. You know I love a craft and wine night."

* * *

LORRAINE WAS STROLLING down the town's square, admiring the spring flowers in full bloom. She had just finished a long shift at the grocery store, and her feet were aching. She couldn't wait to get home and take a long hot bath. As she turned the corner, she saw Christian. She had avoided running into him until now. He held hands with an older woman, and his face lit up when he spotted her. Her heart raced as he got closer, and she couldn't help but feel a mix of emotions — happiness to see him and sadness for what they had lost.

"Hey, Lorraine!" Christian called out, a smile on his face as he walked towards her. "Long time no see."

"Hi, Christian," Lorraine said, trying to sound as composed as possible. "How have you been?"

"I've been good. This is my mom, Gail," Christian said, introducing his mother beside him. "Mom, this is Lorraine."

"Hi, Lorraine," Christian's mother said warmly. "It's so nice to meet you finally."

Lorraine smiled nervously and shook her hand. "It's nice to meet you too, Mrs. Edwards."

"Oh, please, call me Gail," she said, still smiling. "Christian has told me so much about you. He always speaks so highly of you."

Lorraine's heart sank as she shook her hand. Lorraine felt a knot form in her stomach. She didn't know how to respond. She had ended things with Christian, and now she was standing before his mother, who seemed like such a nice person. Lorraine could feel the anxiety building up inside her as she forced a smile and tried to make small talk.

As they chatted, Lorraine discovered that Christian's mother had been a single teenage mother like her. She had struggled but raised her son to be the great man he was today. Lorraine could feel the tears prickling as she listened to Christian's mother tell her story. It was as if she was looking into a mirror, seeing her struggles reflected at her.

It overcame her with emotions. She looked at Christian, who was smiling at her and felt a pang of regret. Maybe she had made a mistake by ending things with him. She missed him but knew she had to stick to her decision.

"I was sorry to hear about Wyatt's injury. How's he doing?" Christian asked.

"How did you know about that?"

"I saw it on social media. I went by the hospital, but since I'm not family and he's a minor, they didn't let me in," Christian replied.

Lorraine nodded, feeling a mix of emotions again. She appreciated that Christian still cared enough to check up on Wyatt, but it also reminded her of the life they used to share. "He's doing better. Thanks for asking. It was a rough couple of weeks, but he's returning to his old self."

"I'm glad to hear that," Christian said, his eyes softening as he looked at her. "Listen, Lorraine. I know we haven't talked since...you know. But I just wanted to say that I still care about you. And I hope we can still be friends."

Lorraine's heart ached as she heard his words. She had

missed him so much, but she also knew that being friends with him would only make it harder for her to move on. "I appreciate that, Christian. But I don't think we can be friends right now. Maybe someday, but not right now."

Christian nodded, looking down at his feet. "Yeah, I understand. Just know I'm here for you if you need anything."

"Thanks, Christian. I appreciate that," Lorraine said, tears pricking at the corners of her eyes. She knew that seeing him would never be easy, but she also knew that she had made the right decision to end things between them. As they said their goodbyes, Lorraine felt a sense of sadness wash over her.

CHAPTER 16

Tiffany was struggling as she pushed the stroller into Cade's office. She took in the impressive space as she stepped in, taking in the new leather chairs, fresh white paint, and modern artwork hanging on the walls. Cade had recently remodeled the office.

"Let me help you," Birdie, Cade's receptionist, said, jumping out of her seat and holding the door open for Tiffany.

"Thanks, Birdie. Sorry to barge in like this, but Cade said he would take the kids for the rest of the day. I have to get to work, and Melanie is running late."

Birdie smiled warmly. "Oh, no problem, sweetie. I love having these three little ones around. They're always such a delight."

Tiffany turned to Ryder. "You be good, okay?"

"Yes mam'," Ryder said.

Tiffany chuckled as she handed over a bag with snacks and toys to Birdie. She turned to leave but paused before the door.

"Oh Birdie, I almost forgot to tell you. I'm pregnant!"

Birdie gasped in excitement. "Oh, honey! That's wonderful news. Congratulations. You and David are going to be great parents. How many kids do you plan to have?"

"I'm not sure yet, but I'm excited to start our own family."

Birdie smiled. "I'm excited for you. I have six of my own and now I'm a grandma of 15!"

"Wow, 15 grandkids. You must be so proud."

"I am. They're all a blessing. There's nothing like being a grandma. It's the best feeling in the world."

Tiffany smiles, imagining the joy of having grandchildren someday.

Birdie turns to the kids and says, "Alright you three, let's go find some fun things to do."

Ryder smiles excitedly, while Harper and Hunter are bundled in their stroller. They look at Birdie, silently observing everything around them.

Tiffany waves goodbye before heading out the door. As she steps out into the crisp mountain air, she can't help but feel excited as she looks down at her stomach. She's still not showing, but she can't wait to look down and see her bump soon.

She gets in her car and drives the short distance to the Inn. The sun is shining brightly, casting a warm glow on the surrounding buildings.

She's nervous as she walks into the Inn. Mrs. Adelman is like a grandmother to her, and she was about to tell her the most important news of her life. She took a deep breath as she approached the front desk counter. Mrs. Adelman glances up from the computer and smiles warmly at Tiffany.

"What brings you here on your day off?"

"Mrs. Adelman, I have something important to tell you. I'm pregnant!"

Mrs. Adelman's eyes widened in surprise, and then she smiles. "Oh, Tiffany, that's wonderful news!" she says, standing up from her desk and giving Tiffany a big hug. "I'm so happy for you."

Tiffany hugs her back, unable to stop smiling. "I'm so grateful to have you in my life."

Mrs. Adelman pulls back from the hug and looks at Tiffany with a twinkle in her eye. "You're going to be a great mother, dear."

Just then, the bell rang, announcing a newcomer. Teddy walked in. He looked at Tiffany and smiled, "Is everything alright?"

Mrs. Adelman turns to her husband and says, "Tiffany has some wonderful news to share with us."

Tiffany smiles and says, "I'm pregnant."

Teddy lets out a whoop of joy. "That's amazing news!" he says, hugging Tiffany.

Tiffany smiles, feeling overjoyed. She knew she and David had a lot of challenges ahead of them. Raising a kid wasn't easy, but they had a group of supportive people that loved them and were looking out for them. This baby was going to be so loved, and she couldn't wait to hold it in her arms.

JASPER SAT on his front porch, thinking how much he cherished each moment with Britney. They had been through so much together, from long-distance struggles to taking breaks from each to Britney leaving her city life to move to Willow Heights. Things had become significantly serious in their relationship. They had talked about their future together and had made plans. Jasper was determined to do everything in his power to make Britney's life everything she ever wished and would be there for her no matter what life threw their way. He loved her and knew she was the love of his life. He had never felt this way about anyone before. She was his opposite but yet they complimented each other. They shared experiences that transcended their personalities and that gave them a deep understanding of each other.

Jasper had been thinking about proposing to Britney but didn't think she was ready for such a big commitment. His top priority was ensuring Britney was happy with her life in Willow Heights. He understood she had changed her lifestyle for him, and he wanted to show her he loved her and that her happiness mattered.

He returned to his cabin, where Britney was sitting on a small desk by the fireplace. She had been working on her social media posts and editing videos to post.

Jasper walked over to Britney and took her hand in his. She turned to face him when he said, "Britney, I've been thinking about our futures together, and I know I want to spend the rest of my life with you. Will you marry me?"

Britney wasn't expecting his proposal. Her eyes widened with surprise and filled with tears. "Yes, I will," she said, jumping up and hugging him.

They held each other for some time. It was such a special and intimate moment. "Are you happy, Britney?" Jasper asked as he looked into her eyes.

"Yes, I am. I love you. I am happy I moved to Willow Heights. I'm where I'm supposed to be. The only thing I wish for is to have a relationship with my mom."

"We'll work on that together. I'm here for you."

Britney knew Jasper loved her deeply and meant what he had said about working together to get her relationship with her mom back on track.

* * *

MARY ELLE WAS VISITING MELANIE, trying to help her find a new preschool and daycare for her young children. The preschool that Melanie visited a few weeks ago didn't have availability for new students to enroll.

Melanie sat on her couch with a list of Willow Heights and Winding Creek preschools. "Mom, I don't know where to start. How do I know which school will best choose the kids?"

"Don't worry about it. Together, we will figure out what to do," Mary Elle said calmly. She didn't miss the stress of finding good schools for kids but understood their importance in children's education.

Just then, Thomas and Cade walked into the living room. They had overheard their conversation.

"I have some good news. That might make your decision easier," Thomas said confidently.

Mary Elle turned to face Thomas. She knew what he was referring to and had been anticipating the moment he would announce it to Melanie.

"David and I have been working on a project at Willow Acres. We turned a cabin into a small preschool and have got permission to open officially."

"Really? That's amazing!" Melanie said with excitement. She knew it would benefit a lot of working moms within Willow Acres and the town. Thomas had been working on this project since Melanie had the twins. He kept it a secret until the town council approved all the paperwork and permits. The time was finally here, and it was now official.

"Yes, it's really happening. We are so blessed to have this opportunity to help you and the other moms at Willow Acres. It's been a long time coming, and now it's time to announce it and start a new school year. We have hired teachers and have everything ready to go," Thomas replied, smiling. Helping others had always made Thomas feel happy.

"We want you to be the first to come to see how everything turned out," Mary Elle said, full of expectation.

"I would love to see it," Melanie said as she put down the list of schools she had been holding onto. She felt relieved of all her anxiety and worry.

Mary Elle, Thomas, and Melanie got into their truck and drove to Willow Acres Preschool. Tiffany and David were there, adding the finishing touches.

"Hi, guys. I wasn't expecting to find you here," Melanie said as she greeted Tiffany and David.

"We were just adding some school supplies that were finally delivered today," David said as he took a box out of his truck.

"So, everyone knew about the preschool except for me?" Melanie asked with a smile.

"Yes, I guess you could say that," Mary Elle replied as she guided Melanie into the new school.

The cabin's layout impressed Melanie, and she was excited for her kids to start the school year at Willow Acres School.

Melanie turned to Mary Elle, Thomas, and David. "Thank you. This means the world to me."

"It's our pleasure. We are happy to help in any way we can," Thomas said with a warm smile.

Melanie expressed her gratitude by hugging them for the support they provided.

CHAPTER 17

*L*orraine and Wyatt arrived early for his physical therapy appointment. The clinic is filled with various equipment and exercise machines. The receptionist greets them with a smile and directs them toward the therapist's office.

Wyatt's therapist Rachel greets them as they walk in. "Hey, Wyatt! Hey Lorraine! How are you guys doing today?"

Wyatt smiles brightly. "I'm feeling great, Rachel! I can't wait to show you how much progress I've made."

Lorraine pats his back. "He's been doing all his exercises and taking his recovery seriously."

Rachel smiles. "That's great to hear. Let's look at your injury and see how we can improve your condition."

As Rachel examines Wyatt's injury, Lorraine watches with a concerned expression. She knows how important basketball is to Wyatt and how devastating the injury was for him.

Rachel makes some notes in Wyatt's file, then turns to them. "Things are looking good. It seems like the injury isn't as bad as we initially thought. You're healing well, and with a few more sessions, you should be back in shape in no time. Let's get started!"

As they begin the session, Wyatt works hard to complete his exercises with Rachel's guidance. He's determined to get back to playing basketball as soon as possible.

"Do you think I'll be able to play in the big game next week?"

Rachel takes a moment to think of her response. "It's still too early to say for sure, Wyatt. But I'm impressed with how much progress you've made. Keep up the good work, and we'll see where you're at next week."

Wyatt nods. "Thanks, Rachel. I will keep working hard and pushing myself to get better."

As they finish the session, Wyatt high-fives Rachel with a big smile.

"Thanks so much, Rachel! I feel like I'm getting stronger every day."

Lorraine grabs her purse. "Thank you, Rachel. We appreciate your hard work and dedication to Wyatt's recovery."

"Wyatt's an impressive guy. He's doing so much better already. He'll be back on the court in no time."

"Thank you so much. I'll do whatever it takes to get back on the court," Wyatt says, beaming.

As they leave the clinic, Wyatt tells Lorraine how happy he is with his progress. He's excited to get back on the court with his team. After today's session, Lorraine feels some of the stress slip away. Wyatt is doing better than they imagined, and his future still looks bright.

"Wyatt, I forgot to mention that I ran into Christian and his mother the other day. He asked how you were doing and wished you a speedy recovery," Lorraine said as she drove home.

"I knew he was worried about me. I saw him at the hospital, but he didn't reach my room," Wyatt replied as he looked out the window.

"Are you excited about going back to school this week? I'm sure all your friends and teammates have been calling and texting you," Lorraine asked as they pulled up to their driveway.

"Yes, I can't wait to see my friends. Daisy texted me when I got injured and apologized on behalf of her boyfriend. He's the kid that hurt me. I told her it's ok, and I'm not holding any grudges," Wyatt shared with his mom.

"That's good. I know it isn't easy to let things go, but I'm proud of you. You're becoming a great man," Lorraine said, smiling proudly. Wyatt was becoming the man she always envisioned him to be. He was kind, smart, hardworking, and dedicated to his family.

"Mom, don't cry," Wyatt said when he noticed Lorraine wiping a tear from her cheek.

"I'm just so proud of you. I can't believe how much God has blessed me with a son like you."

"I'm blessed to have you, Mom. I've seen everything you've gone through and seen how you've reached all your goals, and I know God will help you make all your dreams come true."

"Mary Elle and Thomas have also been instrumental in your growth. I'm so happy they did that for you. I am forever grateful to them."

"I know. They complete our family; without their help, we wouldn't be here."

* * *

Tiffany and David were enjoying their lives as newlyweds. They spent the day running errands and were now on their way home from a very enjoyable dinner at Winding Creek

Ranch. As they drove down a country road, they saw a sign for an animal auction and checked it out.

As they entered the auction, Tiffany was immediately drawn to the animals. Tiffany's eyes grew wide with excitement as she saw the variety of animals on offer. She saw horses, goats, pigs, and cows waiting to be sold to the highest bidder. As they made their way through the rows of cages and pens, Tiffany's heart grew heavy with sadness for the creatures cramped in small spaces, awaiting their fate. As she walked by the pen of cows, one caught her eye. She was malnourished and weak, and Tiffany could see the sadness in her eyes. The cow's coat was dull and patchy.

Tiffany turned to David and said, "We must do something. That cow needs our help."

She knew no one would want to buy her, and she couldn't bear the thought of the poor animal being left behind. Without hesitation, Tiffany walked up to the auctioneer and made a bid for the cow. The other bidders looked at her in surprise. Tiffany was determined to get the cow the help she needed.

At the night's end, they declared Tiffany, the winner of the cow. She and David loaded the cow into their truck and drove her home. They spent hours cleaning her up, brushing her coat, and feeding her.

As they took care of the cow and watched her slowly regain strength, David turned to Tiffany and said, "You know, I won the jackpot when I married you. You're everything I ever wanted in a woman."

Tiffany smiled, feeling grateful for the life they had built together and the animals they would help. They went to sit on the porch and watch the cow, whom they named Maple, graze contentedly in the field.

"You know," Tiffany said, glancing at David with a smile as she rubbed her belly, "I can't wait to be a mom."

David looked at her, his eyes softening. "Me too," he said. "I can't wait to see you as a mom. You're going to be amazing."

Tiffany leaned her head against his chest, feeling his heartbeat steady and strong. "I just can't wait to hold our baby in my arms," she said. "To see their little face."

David hugged her tighter. "I can't wait either," he said. "I can imagine our little ones running around the house, making messes, and driving us crazy."

Tiffany smiled. "Yeah, I can see it now. You, with your endless patience, and me, trying to keep up with them."

They sat there for a little while longer. Dreaming of their future together. Tiffany smiled, feeling the warmth of his embrace. She knew they had a bright future ahead of them and couldn't wait to see what the future held.

* * *

Lorraine pulled up to Mary Elle's house in her beat-up Jeep, her heart racing excitedly. She had just received the news that they had accepted her into the nursing program she had worked so hard for. Her excitement was palpable. She couldn't wait to share the news with everyone she knew. As she exited her car, she took a moment to take a deep breath. The air was crisp and fresh, and she breathed it in deeply.

The mountains had always held a special place in her heart. She had grown up here; this was the only place she had ever called home. Even though her family had moved away, Lorraine couldn't imagine being elsewhere. There was something about the majestic peaks that made her feel at home.

Mary Elle was in her backyard, knee-deep in old boxes and tools as she cleaned out the storage shed. Lorraine could hear her banging around in there, and she knew she wouldn't stop until the job got done. Mary Elle and Thomas were nature lovers; their backyard was a testament to that. Flowers were blooming everywhere, and a small pond in the yard's corner was home to several ducks.

"Mary Elle!" Lorraine called out as she approached her. "I have some amazing news!"

Mary Elle turned around, wiping the sweat from her brow. "What's going on?" she asked.

"I got in!" Lorraine exclaimed, smiling from ear to ear. "I got into the nursing program!"

Mary Elle's eyes widened in excitement, and she ran over to hug Lorraine. "That's amazing, Lorraine! I'm so proud of you! You're going to be an amazing nurse."

Lorraine got emotional just reflecting on her journey. Not long ago, she would've laughed if someone told her she would be on her way to being a nurse.

"Mary Elle, I don't think I could have done this without you," Lorraine said, her voice filled with emotion.

"Of course, you could have, sweetie."

"You've always been there for me," Lorraine continued. "You've always believed in me and encouraged me to follow my dreams, even when I didn't believe in myself. And Thomas, too. You both have done so much for me and Wyatt, and I just wanted to thank you. You're the first person I wanted to tell."

Mary Elle smiled, her eyes shining with warmth. "Lorraine, you don't have to thank us. We've always believed in you because we know how capable you are. Thomas and I have always been happy to help you and Wyatt in any way we can. You are family to us."

Lorraine felt a lump form in her throat at Mary Elle's words. She had always known they cared about her and Wyatt, but hearing her say they were family touched her more than anyone could ever know.

"I know," Lorraine said, her voice thick with emotion. "You've helped me achieve my dream of becoming a nurse, and I'll never forget that."

Wyatt arrived just as they finished their conversation, and it thrilled him to hear the news. As they all sat down on the porch steps to celebrate, Lorraine couldn't help but take in the beauty of the mountains surrounding them.

The sun was setting now, casting a golden light over everything in its path. Mary Elle brought out some sweet tea, and they all sipped on it as they chatted about Lorraine's future.

Wyatt was excited about his mom's new career path. "You're going to be a great nurse, Mom," he said, his eyes shining with pride.

Lorraine smiled at him, feeling grateful for his unwavering support. "Thank you, honey," she said. "I couldn't have done it without you."

As the sun set, the three of them continued to talk and laugh, enjoying each other's company.

CHAPTER 18

Mary Elle knocked on the door of Tiffany and David's house. Her heart was heavy, knowing that her daughter was in pain. She had just found out that Tiffany had suffered a miscarriage, and she couldn't wait any longer to see her. She dropped everything she had to do and came as soon as possible.

David answered the door, looking tired and worn out. "Hi, Mary Elle," he said softly. "Thanks for coming."

Mary Elle gave him a warm hug. "Of course, dear. How's Tiffany doing?" she asked, concern written all over her face.

David shook his head, his eyes filling with tears. "She's not doing well. She's been in bed all day, hardly talking at all."

Mary Elle took a deep breath and said a prayer as she walked to the bedroom. Tiffany looked so small and vulnerable, curled up under the blankets. Mary Elle gently stroked her hair, trying to keep her own tears at bay.

"Tiffany, honey," Mary Elle said softly, "I'm here. Thomas is here too."

Thomas nodded from the other side of the room. His eyes showed the same worry as his wife's.

Tiffany didn't respond at first, but she eventually sat up. "I'm sorry," she whispered. "I just don't know what to say."

Mary Elle took Tiffany's hand in hers. "You don't have to say anything, sweetie. We're here for you."

Thomas nodded. "We love you, and we'll get through this together."

Tiffany managed a small smile. She excused herself to use the restroom, and as she left the room, David turned to Mary, Elle, and Thomas.

"I love her so much, but I don't know what to do," he admitted, his voice breaking. "Tiffany's pushing me away, and I don't know how to help her. She won't let me in."

Thomas put a comforting arm around his shoulders. "It's okay. Tiffany's hurting right now, and she needs time to heal. Just be there for her, love her, and support her. That's all you can do."

"Sometimes the best thing we can do for someone is to be there for them, even if they don't want to talk," Mary Elle said. "Just let her know you love her and are there for her."

David nodded, feeling a sense of relief, knowing that he had them to lean on. Together, they would help Tiffany heal from the pain of losing their baby.

Tiffany had been quietly standing by the door, listening to their conversation.

"I'm sorry," she said. "I know I've been pushing you away. I don't know how to deal with this."

David wrapped his arms around her, pulling her close. "It's okay," he said. "We'll get through this together."

LORRAINE WAS ALWAYS IN A RUSH, but she was running behind today. She had an important meeting with Wyatt's school counselor and didn't want to be late. She stopped by the Busy

Bee Coffee Shop to grab a cup of coffee. As she was hurrying inside, she bumped into someone.

"I'm so sorry," Lorraine said as she looked up to see Christian smiling.

"It's okay. Are you alright?" Christian asked.

The encounter surprised Lorraine, but she quickly regained her composure. "Yes, I'm fine. Thank you."

Christian noticed Lorraine was hurrying and offered to pay for her coffee. Christian asks Lorraine how she's been as they wait for their coffee. She tells him she just got accepted into the nursing program.

Christian's eyes lit up with pride. "I'm so proud of you, Lorraine. I always knew you had it in you," Christian says, placing a hand on her shoulder.

Lorraine felt her eyes sting. She had missed Christian so much; it felt good to be back in his presence.

When Wendy gives them their coffee, they walk to the town square, where they sit on a bench and continue their conversation. Wyatt is supposed to be meeting her in the square any minute now.

"I'm sorry for ending things," she says, her voice cracking. "I did it out of fear."

"Fear of what," Christian asks, concerned.

"Of not being good enough for you," Lorraine admitted. "You're so accomplished, and it scared me you would eventually think I wasn't good enough."

Christian shakes his head. His eyes softened as he took her hands. "I would never think that," he says firmly. "I love you for who you are."

Lorraine felt relief wash over her as she looked into Christian's eyes. She leaned in, and they shared a sweet kiss, their lips meeting as if they had never been apart. They stay seated on the bench and continue talking.

Just then, Wyatt shows up.

"Hey, Mom," he says and quickly hugs her. He then turns to Christian, gives him a fist bump, and says, "Hey Christian! Long time no see."

Christian smiles and pats Wyatt on the back. "How have you been, champ?"

Wyatt's face lights up as he tells him he's in the clear to play basketball again. "The biggest game of the season is coming up. Will you be there?"

"Of course, I wouldn't miss it for the world," Christian says, making Wyatt beam excitedly.

Lorraine feels her heart warm at their interaction. She fell in love with Christian because of the support he showed Wyatt.

* * *

It had been a week since Tiffany's miscarriage. Mary Elle and Thomas went to Tiffany's house to check on her. Everyone was still reeling from the emotional trauma of the unexpected event. Tiffany had been trying hard to seem like she was back to normal, but Mary Elle knew it was still taking a toll on her.

"How are you feeling, darling?" Mary Elle said as she reached out her hand, pulling Tiffany in for a hug.

"I don't know. I'm not sure what I'm supposed to feel. I'm sad and scared," Tiffany said as she leaned her head onto Mary Elle's shoulder.

"We are worried about you," Thomas said as he sat down next to them with concern written on his face.

Tiffany looked up and said, "I know you guys are all worried about me. I need a little time to process everything."

"I know, honey. I can see you are being strong and trying to handle this alone. We want you to know that we are here for you. David is also here for you and worried about you," Mary Elle said as she squeezed Tiffany's hand.

"We are here for you in case you need anything," Thomas said, nodding in agreement. "Whatever it is, we are here for you and David."

Tiffany wiped tears from her eyes and deeply breathed, "I feel so many things right now. I appreciate you guys coming over and being here with me."

"We will take it one day at a time. There's no rush to get back to normal just yet. Healing takes time, and we are here for you," Mary Elle said as she hugged Tiffany tight.

"Thanks, Mom. I know I can always count on you and Thomas," Tiffany said.

"We love you, Tiff," Thomas nodded, squeezing her hand. "I know you're in pain now, and nothing we say or do can take it away. I want you to know that no matter what, you should never give up hope. Although you find yourself in a situation we never imagined you being in, and you feel lost and alone. Don't lose hope. Things will get better, and you will find your way out of this darkness."

"Thanks, Thomas," Tiffany said.

"We called Ruby and Michael to tell them. I hope you don't mind. Your father and Barb also know and have said they will visit soon," Mary Elle shared, hoping Tiffany wouldn't get upset about her sharing the sad news.

"It's ok. I was going to call them but didn't find the strength to utter the words out loud," Tiffany said with a sigh.

Mary Elle and Thomas exchanged a look of relief and hoped that Tiffany would understand how much they loved her and were there to help her in any way she needed.

As Mary Elle and Thomas drive down the winding mountain roads, Mary Elle sits in the passenger seat of their pickup truck; her arms folded tightly across her chest. The sound of the engine is the only noise. They are both lost in their own thoughts.

Suddenly, Mary Elle breaks the silence, "Thomas, I can't stop thinking about Tiffany. I'm really worried about her. I don't know how she's going to cope."

Thomas takes his eyes off the road for a moment as he glances at Mary Elle. "It's understandable to be worried about her. Tiffany has been through a lot, but she's a strong person, and all she needs is a little time."

"I know," Mary Elle said. "But what if she doesn't? What if she can't cope with it?"

Thomas turns onto their street and pulls into their driveway. He puts the truck in the park and turns to face Mary Elle. "Listen to me," he says. "Tiffany is one of the strongest people I know. She's been through a lot and always comes out on the other side. This is no different."

Mary Elle looks at Thomas, her eyes searching his face. "But what if this is more than she can handle?"

Thomas reaches out and takes Mary Elle's hand. "Then we'll get her the help she needs," he says. "But right now, all we can do is to be there for her. Listen to her. Support her. That's what she needs most. We can't keep worrying about everything that can go wrong and expecting the worst. You're going to drive yourself crazy."

Mary Elle nods. "You're right," she says. "Thanks for always knowing what to say."

Thomas smiles at her. "That's what I'm here for," he says.

CHAPTER 19

Lorraine and Christian arrived at the high school gym for Rosie's cheerleading competition. They were both dressed casually, Lorraine wore a white t-shirt and jeans, while Christian wore a blue polo with khaki shorts. Wyatt was in the bleachers with his friends when Lorraine and Christian arrived.

"Hey, mom, hey, Christian," Wyatt said with a smile.

As the competition started, Lorraine and Christian joined the other parents in cheering for the teams. Wyatt sat between them, smiling proudly and cheering for Rosie.

After the competition, Lorraine and Christian went to the gym floor to congratulate Rosie on her performance. They also met her parents.

"Hi, I'm Lorraine, Wyatt's mom, and this is my boyfriend, Christian," Lorraine said, extending her hand for a handshake.

"Nice to meet you both," Mrs. Peterson replied, shaking their hands. "Rosie talks about you all the time."

They exchanged pleasantries while Rosie finished talking

with her friends. The Petersons were friendly and outgoing. Lorraine and Christian felt at ease with them.

"There's a great Italian place just down the street," Mr. Peterson said. "We'd love to treat you all."

Lorraine and Christian exchanged a glance, then nodded in agreement. They didn't have any other plans for the night, and they knew how much it meant for Wyatt that they got to know Rose's parents.

Over dinner, they talked about school, sports, and hobbies. Lorraine really enjoyed the Peterson's company. She'd been worried that they wouldn't get along, but they were down to earth. Rosie and Wyatt shared their college plans, and Lorraine noticed a shift in the atmosphere. When the young couple excused themselves to talk with friends outside, Mrs. Peterson expressed her concerns.

"They're so young," she said, shaking her head. "I worry that they're getting too serious too fast."

Lorraine felt thrown off. She hadn't really thought of their relationship that way. Was she right? Were they getting too serious? What did that even mean?

"I understand your concerns. I think that if they're happy and keeping up with their grades, we should let them enjoy their youth."

The Petersons didn't seem to like that response, but they said nothing else. As the evening drew to a close, Lorraine and Christian said their goodbyes and drove home. Lorraine couldn't stop thinking about the comment. She had to talk to Wyatt and figure out what was going on.

"Do you think they're right?" Lorraine asked, turning to face Christian.

"Right, about what?"

"About Wyatt and Rosie getting too serious, too fast."

Christian took a moment to think about his response. "I don't know, Lorraine. They might be right," he said. "Wyatt and Rosie have been spending a lot of time together, and he seems serious about her. Maybe we should talk to him about it."

Lorraine stared out the window as she mulled over the conversation with the Petersons. She had dismissed their comments at the time. Shining they were just being overprotective of their daughter. But now, she couldn't help but wonder if they had a point.

Had she missed something? Had she been so wrapped up in her own life that she hadn't paid enough attention to what was going on with Wyatt?

* * *

THE BIG GAME day had finally arrived. Wyatt had been so worried about not being well enough to play, but Rachel, his therapist, had ok'd him to play. He was so excited he couldn't even sleep the night before. Rosie had made a new cheer for him. She was the head cheerleader of Willow Heights High, and the squad came up with new dance moves and cheers. They also got new banners and pompoms to make the basketball team's new uniform. The whole town was excited to see the game. They even made flyers to make sure everyone in Willow Heights knew about the game.

Christian knocked on the door. He was holding a gigantic bouquet of red roses with a small card.

"Chris, wow," Lorraine said as she opened the door and saw the roses.

"They are for you. Here's the card," Christian said as he handed her the roses and card. He was feeling nervous but excited. They had just gotten back together, and he didn't want to rush things with Lorraine in case she was feeling doubt.

"Thank you, I love them," Lorraine said as she welcomed

Christian into the house and placed the roses on her coffee table. She read the card, and it read: I love you. You are everything I ever wanted, and I wouldn't change anything about you. Lorraine, you are strong, loving, kind, and beautiful. You are more than enough for me. I'm so proud of you. All your hard work has paid off, and there's no reason to doubt yourself ever again.

Reading Christian's words brought tears of joy to Lorraine's eyes. She loved him. Now she understood that her worth was her own. She had come this far with the help of others, but they did not hand her success to her. She worked for it, and she was at peace with herself.

"I mean every word I wrote on that card," Christian said as he walked over to Lorraine. She was sniffling and wiping a tear from her cheek.

"I know. It touched me." They hugged for a moment until they realized it was time to get to the gymnasium for the game.

Lorraine gave Wyatt's room door a small knock and poked her.

"Are you ready to win?" Lorraine asked Wyatt excitedly. She was his number one fan. Wyatt loved her enthusiasm and support.

"Yes, I am!" Wyatt roared.

"That's right, and you're going to win!" Christian chimed in. He had shown up at the house before the game to show support and make sure Wyatt was mentally and emotionally ready to play. The practice had been challenging for Wyatt because he was worried. He would overdo it and not be ready for the game.

"You're feeling good?" Lorraine asked Wyatt, making sure he wasn't in pain.

"I'm fine, Mom. I feel good. No pain. If I feel pain, I'll let the coach know," Wyatt replied as he took his sneakers to the sofa to put them on.

Lorraine smiled as she watched him. Her little boy was all grown up now.

The gym was packed with excited fans, parents, and students, all waiting for the start of the big basketball game. Wyatt and his team were warming up on the court, and the tension was palpable. As the game began, the crowd erupted into cheers.

The announcer came on the speakers. "Ladies and gentlemen, welcome to the biggest game of the season! This is a crucial game for both teams, and scouts from major universities are in attendance. Let's give it up for your favorite team!"

The crowd roared as the teams took the court.

The game was intense, with both teams playing their best. The score was close through, and the tension was high. Wyatt was playing his heart out, dribbling past the defender and making amazing shots. Mary Elle and Lorraine held hands, their nerves all over the place.

As the clock ticked down, the game became even more intense. The crowd was on their feet, cheering for their hometown team. Wyatt and his team were determined to win and played with all their might. The other team was also strong, but Wyatt's team was relentless.

Wyatt tied the score with only a few seconds left on the clock. The tension in the gym was palpable as Wyatt dribbled the ball down the court. Wyatt moved, tricking the defender and launching the ball toward the basket. The ball hit the rim, bounced up, and gracefully fell through the net. The crowd exploded into cheers as the buzzer sounded, signaling the end of the game.

The excitement filled the air as the game ended. Wyatt played his best game, impressing the coach.

"What an amazing game!" Thomas said excitedly as he greeted Wyatt after the game.

"Thanks, I tried my best. I was worried about going overboard, but I'm glad I didn't," Wyatt replied, beaming from their school victory.

"Amazing game. Your dedication and love for the sport is evident," Mary Elle said as she appeared from the side of the court.

"I'm glad you guys made it and enjoyed the game. It was very intense," Wyatt said, smiling widely.

"We are very proud of you," Cade said as he squeezed Wyatt's shoulder.

"There he is," Christian said as he and Lorraine walked hand in hand toward the group.

"I see you guys have made up," Mary Elle said joyfully.

"We worked things out. I'm glad we are getting our second chance," Christian said as he kissed Lorraine.

"It's all about communication," Mary Elle said as she hugged them both.

Rosie comes running to congratulate her favorite basketball player, "Congratulations on your big win!"

"Thanks. You and the squad did an amazing job of getting the crowd going," Wyatt replied. He was proud of Rosie. She had come a long way too. She wasn't always this confident and outgoing, but cheering had helped her, and it was something she enjoyed.

* * *

Sienna, Kyle, and Liam were driving to visit her adoptive parents in Helen. Sienna's mom, Madeline, had completed her cancer treatment and was looking forward to meeting Kyle and his son, Liam.

As they drove through the winding mountain roads,

Sienna shared childhood experiences with Kyle and Liam, who listened intently, fascinated by her stories.

When they arrived at Sienna parent's house, Madeline, who had been sitting on her front porch awaiting their arrival, greeted them. Frank, Sienna's adoptive father, was at work. Her adoptive parents had separated but had since reconciled and were back together.

Madeline hugged Sienna tightly, happy to see her and to meet her new boyfriend, Kyle, and his son, Liam.

Madeline led them inside the house and offered them sweet iced tea while they sat in the living room and talked for a while before settling in. The house had rustic décor with modern appliances. It was a nice, big house.

Frank arrived as they settled in, and Madeline made dinner for them. Frank and Kyle discussed fishing and hunting while Sienna and Madeline finished setting the dinner table with Liam's help. It felt great to bring home Kyle and Liam. Sienna had been dreaming of this moment for some time. She wanted to share some of her favorite childhood hangout spots with them and spend time with Madeline and Frank. Her sister, Olivia, wasn't in town but had promised to make it while they were still in Helen. Olivia was still in college and worked part-time. It was final exam week, and she had been busy studying.

After dinner, they sat outside on the back porch, wrapped in blankets with hot cocoa, watching the stars twinkle. Sienna felt content to see everyone getting along and having a great time together.

Madeline cleared her throat quietly, and everyone turned to face her. "Sienna, your father and I have wanted to give you something to show how much we love you and how proud we are of you. You've become a beautiful, strong, intelligent woman, and we couldn't be prouder of you."

She handed Sienna a small box. Sienna's chest tightened

with expectation. She opened the box carefully, revealing a golden bracelet with her initials carved into it.

Sienna's eyes swelled with tears. It was such a beautiful bracelet and gesture. She knew her adoptive parents loved her and had always been there for her, but this tender gift made her feel loved.

"Thanks, Mom and Dad," Sienna said as she stood up to give them a big bear hug.

"We love you, and just like your mom said, we are very proud of you," Frank said, holding back tears of love.

Once Sienna sat back next to Kyle, he wrapped his arms around her and whispered, "I'm happy to be here sharing this experience with you."

The following day, Sienna and Madeline woke early to make a big breakfast for everyone. They had a day of hiking ahead of them and wanted to make the best of their time while visiting.

After breakfast, they started their hike. The day was gorgeous; the weather was perfect; it wasn't too chilly or hot today. The flowers were blooming, and the sky was clear—there was no chance of rain today. The trail wasn't easy, but it had a magnificent top view, making it worth the rugged terrain. They had a lunch picnic at the top of the mountain and took several photos. Liam enjoyed the hike and took a quick nap before they headed back down the trail.

Frank turned to Kyle, saying, "Sienna is an extraordinary girl, and we are glad to see her this happy with you."

Kyle smiled as he looked at Sienna, walking a few steps behind them with Madeline and Liam. "She's the best thing that has ever happened to me."

When they returned home, they had a nice relaxing night of playing board games and cooking their favorite chili recipe. They all sat at the table, playing, laughing, and enjoying each other's company. Kyle hugged Sienna, kissed her forehead, and whispered, "I love you so much. This has been an amazing weekend."

Sienna's heart soared. She felt extremely loved and blessed to have her adoptive parents, Kyle and Liam. She had everything and everyone she needed in her life. Life was beyond anything she had ever expected.

CHAPTER 20

It was Sunday again, and Mary Elle had invited her kids over for dinner, along with Rita and Bob, Sienna and Kyle, and Lorraine and Christian. It was the first time Christian could attend Mary Elle's Sunday dinner. Wyatt was happy to have him join them. Melanie, Cade, and the kids arrived late, just in time to start dinner.

Mary Elle elegantly decorated the dining room. Thomas had made a wooden picnic table for the kids, next to the adult dining table. The air smelled of freshly baked bread and roasted chicken.

Mary Elle greeted everyone as they arrived. Lorraine was beaming with joy. Christian was finally joining them, and she couldn't be happier.

"Welcome, Christian. It is great to have you over for dinner finally," Mary Elle said as she greeted them.

"Thank you for having me. I'm excited to be here," Christian said as they entered the living room.

"Lorraine, I'm so happy to see you. You look gorgeous," Mary Elle said as she hugged Lorraine, who was like a daughter to her.

"Thanks, Mary Elle," Lorraine said, smiling brightly.

As all the guests sat down at the dining table, conversation flowed.

"How's work going?" Thomas asked Cade.

"It's going well. Thanks for asking," Cade said, smiling.

"I heard you remodeled the office," David asked.

"Yeah, it was time for a little facelift," Cade replied.

Soon the conversation turned lighthearted.

"Guys, what do you call an angry carrot?" David said, trying not to laugh.

"What?" Cade asked, unsure what the answer would be to this dad's joke.

"A steamed veggie," David said, bursting into laughter.

Everyone laughed, and soon everyone started telling their best dad jokes. Dinner was fun, and everyone was having a great time.

IT HAD BEEN two years since Lorraine had walked into Christian's life. Although they hadn't been dating for long, he was sure she was the woman he wanted to spend the rest of his life with. He also knew he had to get Wyatt's permission before proposing to Lorraine.

One Saturday morning, Christian took Wyatt out fishing. They hiked through dense rocky terrain until they reached a serene lake between two steep hills. They sat on the dock, surrounded by calm water and chirping birds. They stayed put, waiting for a bite.

"Hey, Wyatt," Christian said. "I want to talk to you about something."

Wyatt put down his fishing rod and turned to face Christian. "What is it?"

"I love your mom, Wyatt. And I want to ask her to marry

me. But before I do that, I want your permission first. What do you say?"

"Really?"

Christian nodded. "Yes, really. I love your mom and want to spend the rest of my life with her. I know how important you are to her, and I want to make sure you're okay with it before I ask her."

Wyatt looked at Christian briefly, then looked away, his brow furrowed. He stared at the water, deep in thought. Christian waited patiently, giving Wyatt space to think.

Finally, Wyatt looked at Christian and said, "Yes, I really like you, Christian. You make my mom happy, and that's all that matters to me. I always wanted my mom to find love and happiness. I think you're a good guy."

Christian smiled, relieved. "Thank you, Wyatt. That means a lot to me."

Wyatt smiled back. "You have my permission to marry my mom. I think you're a great guy, and I know you'll take good care of her."

"Thank you, Wyatt. I promise always to take care of your mom and to be there for both of you."

Christian and Wyatt talked about their shared love of the outdoors and the adventures they wanted to take as a family as they continued fishing. Christian knew he had found the right woman and family to spend his life with.

They spent a few hours fishing and talking, enjoying the peacefulness of the mountains. The sun set behind the mountains, casting a warm orange glow across the sky. Christian reeled in his fishing rod and turned to Wyatt. "Let's head back, buddy. Your mom will wonder where we are."

Wyatt nodded and packed up his fishing gear. As they returned to the car, Christian felt a sense of excitement and nervousness. He knew he had Wyatt's blessing but still had to ask Lorraine to marry him. He imagined himself, Lorraine, and Wyatt taking more trips like this, making memories, and cherishing each other's company.

Later that evening, Christian took Lorraine to dinner at a nice restaurant. They enjoyed a delicious meal and talked about their future. Christian got down on one knee as they finished their dessert, took Lorraine's hand, and looked into her eyes.

"Lorraine, I love you more than anything in this world," Christian said. "You make me feel complete, and I can't imagine spending my life without you. Wyatt gave me his blessing today to ask you to marry me. I know I've found my home with you and Wyatt, and I hope you will say yes."

Lorraine's eyes widened in surprise and joy. Tears welled up in her eyes as she looked at Christian. "Yes, Christian, I will marry you," she said.

Christian felt a rush of happiness and relief as he slipped the ring on Lorraine's finger. They hugged each other tightly, and Christian whispered in her ear," I can't wait to spend the rest of my life making you happy."

Lorraine smiled as she reflected on her relationship with Christian. She thought about all the times she had given up hope and convinced herself she would never find love and that she wasn't worthy. She knew not everyone was lucky enough to get a second chance at love. Lorraine knew that many people out there had been hurt and had given up hope, but she wanted them to know that it was never too late to love again.

She smiled as she watched a couple walk by, holding hands and laughing together. She knew they had probably been through their struggles, but they had found each other and were now experiencing the beauty of love.

Loraine glanced at Christian, her heart full. She knew there were so many more beautiful moments to come in their love story, and she was ready to embrace them with an open heart.

THANK you for reading Second Chances in Willow Heights. I hope you enjoyed it! Your support means the world to me. The **last** book in the series is No Place Like Willow Heights.

Printed in Great Britain
by Amazon